REA

ACPL IT

S0-DRZ-899

3 1833 024

F

DISCARDED

Moore, Craig.
A sailor's valentine

A Sailor's Valentine

A Sailor's Valentine

Stories

Craig Moodie

St. Martin's Press New York

These stories have been published—some of them in slightly different form—in the following publications. My thanks to the editors for permission to reprint them in this collection.

Nantucket Journal: "The Shearwater" and "Child in the Shoals"
Northeast: "The Dream of the Whistling Pig"

A S A I L O R ' S V A L E N T I N E .

Copyright © 1994 by Craig Moodie. All rights reserved. Printed in the United States of America. No part of this book may be used or reproduced in any manner whatsoever without written permission except in the case of brief quotations embodied in critical articles or reviews. For information, address St. Martin's Press, 175 Fifth Avenue, New York, N.Y. 10010.

DESIGN BY JUDITH A. STAGNITTO

Library of Congress Cataloging–in–Publication Data

Moodie, Craig.
    A sailor's valentine / Craig Moodie.
      p.   cm.
    ISBN 0-312-11053-7
    1. Sea stories—Massachusetts—Cape Cod.   I. Title.
PS3563.O547S25   1994
813'.54—dc20   94-1998
                                                    CIP

First Edition: May 1994

10 9 8 7 6 5 4 3 2 1

To Ellen, silver moonlight, sweet breeze,
without whom I'd be lost at sea.

CONTENTS

THE DREAM OF
THE WHISTLING PIG

Just let me close them. Let me close my eyes and sleep.

Ray Hill forced himself to keep his eyes open. They were hot and prickly and his eyelids quivered, but he managed to squint up at the orange radar screen and glance at the cherry red numbers of the loran. Then he settled his eyes on the yawing compass.

Can't let myself sleep, he thought, mesmerized by the sway of the compass, by the modulating roar of the diesel. He felt the boat slow as it climbed up one face of a swell. The boat seemed like it was burrowing into the wave for a good night's sleep, and Hill let his eyelids droop.

But then the boat topped the wave and sped into the trough.

Got to stay awake.

Through the pilothouse windows, he saw the flashflash, flash-flashflash of the Great Round Shoal buoy, three miles away.

I've got to get a breath of air, he thought. *Go aft, take a leak, wake up.*

Check the radar, the loran, the compass. Over and over and over. Every half hour, mark down the loran numbers and move the little red-knobbed pins, like mini gearshifts, on the chart to mark the boat's progress toward the fishing grounds, thirty miles beyond where they were now, in Nantucket Shoals, a zone of rips, whirlpools, and freakish seas.

Two more hours of this, he thought. *Two more hours before I wake up Harry.*

He opened the door to the deck and moved out onto the afterdeck, forcing himself to think of every move, even though the boat took the swells methodically, gracefully.

The moment he gulped in the air, he felt refreshed. The boat cutting through the water made a sizzling sound and cold spray tingled against his face. He braced one knee against the gunwale, the other against the fish box. Aiming at the aftermost scupper, he peed directly on the deck.

He yawned and tipped his head upward to gaze at the archipelagoes of stars. There were the Pleiades and Cassiopeia. There was Orion. And over there the Big Dipper, which he once had told his three-year-old daughter always poured out clam chowder around this part of the world. He thought of his wife, Judy, asleep back home.

Bet she's on my side, snoring, he thought, and a smile crossed his lips.

A shooting star flashed across the eastern sky like a needle stitched through black fabric. He finished and zipped up, glancing at the phosphorescence in the boat's wake.

As he turned back to the pilothouse, something from beyond the long eastern horizon found the boat: a wave that had been traveling over the dark seas from a distant storm, a wake that had been speeding over the ocean from an unseen freighter or tanker, a hand from an invisible force. This force, this something in the form of a contrary wave, nudged the boat as it crested a swell, skewed the rhythm, pitched the port side of the boat up, and sent Hill somersaulting into the sea.

The split second he surfaced, he began thrashing wildly after the departing boat. He didn't pause to think. He didn't yell, but his heart beat *Oh God Oh God Oh God.* All he could make out against the starry sky were the boat's red, green, and white running lights. The engine, which a blink in time before had been an enveloping roar, was now reduced to a whisper, an exhalation.

Then the running lights disappeared behind the hulk of a large swell. They reappeared, but smaller now, more distant.

Hill stopped thrashing and started treading water. He looked around him. He saw the dark lips of the waves rise up to kiss the stars. He bobbed up with one to its crest, its small, sizzling whitecap wrapping around his shoulders like a shawl. He pedaled in the dark water and watched the lights of the boat appear and disappear, appear and disappear, appear and disappear. And disappear.

Oh God, Oh God, Oh God, he thought, feeling just beneath the tips of his toes the immensity of the depths beneath him. He wanted to rise up on the surface and run after the boat. But he felt a force drawing him downward, the huge blackness beneath him like another magnetic field, the force of depth.

"HARRY!" he called out over the waves. "HARR-REEEEE!"

The place where the boat's lights had vanished was beneath Orion. The three bright stars that formed Orion's belt were like the pins fixed to the chart, all three in a tilted row.

The water was icy. He knew he would not last long. Already his fingers felt pickled. His jaw trembled.

He thought of the feel of the boat. God, to have that back! To feel the soundness of wood, the vibration of the engine that he so often complained about. To hear the roar of the diesel. To see Harry's weather-cracked and sleep-swollen face, to hear him cursing and laughing, to curse him for his superstitious ways, like the way he spat on bait now and then for good luck when they trawled for halibut or the way he switched off the automatic pilot near a buoy in case of "electrical disturbances." And he remembered the electric bill. Had he paid it? Had Judy? Whether it mattered or not, it lodged in his thoughts, until he rose over a swell and saw the emptiness of the night ocean.

The boat, the boat: gone.

Give it back to me! he roared to himself. *Give it all back. I'll do anything to get it all back. Anything, anything. Please.*

A swell swept underneath him. As he was lifted up, he saw flashflash, flashflashflash. *I'm here, signaled the buoy. Your last chance.* Then the light was obliterated by a wave.

But Hill had marked it with the star pins of Orion.

Furiously he began to swim toward the stars, furiously he panted, furiously he fought over the crests and through the troughs.

He stopped to get his bearings. He searched for the light. *Where'd it go? Have I been swept by it?*

Then, like the brief flare of a match lit in a hurricane, the buoy flashed from a different direction, to the east.

Hill thrashed off after it, but after a few strokes, he felt himself wearing down. He pulled up, gasping and spitting seawater.

Where's the light, damn it, where'd it go?

Another glimpse of it, behind him now, another desperate thrashing.

He swam after it, swam and swam, and when he looked up, the buoy was behind him again, and he choked on the water, and he swam after it, and then it was behind him again, and the stars began shifting and spinning, and the light was flashing, and he wanted to shut his eyes, and he gagged on the water, and the flashing, the flashing, the flashing.

His first thought when he woke up in his bunk was that he'd better not tell Judy about the dream, because she worried enough about him going to sea as it was. It was not the kind of dream to repeat around anyone, especially fishermen, whose ancient superstitions forbade them even whistling or saying the word *pig* before heading off to sea.

He looked up from his bunk and saw the stars and the flash of the buoy in the porthole. Ah, how wonderful to wake up before it was time for your watch, knowing that you had maybe an entire hour of delicious rest before you had to take the helm! Maybe he would even go topside to razz Harry about having to stay up and steer, then return to the bunk and savor the sleeping bag and watch the stars rock in the porthole till he dropped off again.

It was the stars themselves that made him sit up. Something was wrong. The same stars should have stayed visible in the porthole. But different constellations kept appearing.

We are going in circles, thought Hill.

He thrust the sleeping bag aside, groped for the light switch, couldn't find it, tripped up through the companionway, and arrived in his stocking feet in the pilothouse.

"Harry?" he called out in the diesel roar. "Harry, where are you?"

Everything was as it should have been. The loran displayed its numbers. The radar screen glowed. The compass swayed.

Everything was as it should have been, except that the helm was turning itself, unencumbered by the automatic pilot, unencumbered by a human hand, spinning itself, turning the boat in circles.

And through the pilothouse windows, the flashflash, flashflashflash of the buoy.

REPORT FROM
POLLOCK RIP

The faint heaviness you feel from the centrifugal force of a turning boat woke me out of a dense sleep. My body was leaning slightly to the starboard when my eyes cleared and focused on the bright overhead light on the ceiling. The engine made a vaguely labored torquing sound. I heard the drive shaft cavitating, something it did on a tight starboard turn—one of the *Silent Lady*'s idiosyncrasies. None of this made any sense to me. I felt all the sensations, and yet they meant nothing. They couldn't be real. We were on our way home. We had no reason to be changing course, turning around, heading back out into the storm. I lay there, exhausted, half-dreaming, staring at the light. I craned my neck to ask Christo, but his bunk was empty.

I slid out of the bunk and went topside. Chuck was still at the helm, and Christo was digging some thick line and buoys out of the port lazaret.

"What's up?" I yelled over the engine noise.

"Distress call," said Chuck, his eyes on the compass. "Just came over the radio."

I looked at the compass and we were indeed headed directly back into the open ocean and the storm we had just run from. My pulse jumped to a new register.

"Gordie, get the inflatable, the life jackets, and the survival suits out," said Chuck.

"Should we put on the suits?"

"No, they're in case we find anybody to save."

I pulled the crimson suits out of the locker and laid them on the deck. Supposedly, if you went overboard with a survival suit on, they were warm and buoyant enough to keep you alive for a few hours, rather than the minutes the Atlantic would give you if you went in the drink with only your dirty long johns on. You could, conceivably, put one on in the water. I would have felt better with my crimson space suit on at that very second, even though we were only nearing Monomoy Point.

Christo had gotten three coils of line with life jackets attached to them neatly arranged by the hauling door. We were close enough to the Point so that the residual swells were lifting us and then letting us slide steeply down their faces into the troughs, giving us a taste of things to come. I got the inflatable raft out and set it beside the coils. Chuck flipped the radio from the emergency channel to get the weather. It sounded even worse than before: gale-force winds coming due east, with rapidly falling temperatures and rain changing to sleet or snow by midnight. It was about ten o'clock.

When he flipped back to the emergency frequency, we cut into a voice, a crackly, frantic voice, one that was barely understandable for its Portuguese accent.

". . . listing . . . taking on seas" was all I made out through the static and his accent. Then he gave his position and said he had two pumps working in the bilge.

"Who is he?" I said to Chuck.

"The *Doris L.* Some dragger from Fairhaven."

"Where are they?"

"Pollock Rip."

Chuck got on the radio to say that we were in their area and we were assisting.

Vicious place, Pollock Rip. Rips in general are no place for a vessel in a gale in the middle of February. One time when I was crewing on a jig boat, the *Pooh Bah,* we had steamed through a booming rip on Orion Shoal when the wind was light and variable. It was November. We plowed into the face of it okay, but once we got inside the really churned-up stuff, the *Pooh Bah* spun right around, three times, like a weather vane in a tornado. In a gale, the big seas would cover over some of the chop, but the rip itself would be as riotous as if someone was holding a bottle of water and shaking it.

A dragger is a big vessel, maybe even running eighty, a hundred feet, better able to withstand a bad storm than us. Something had gone wrong for them. No matter how you looked at it, Pollock Rip was no place for the *Doris L.* It was no place for the *Silent Lady.* It was no place for humans. It belonged to the wind, the waves, the tides, and fate. But it was getting closer.

When we rounded the point, out of the lee of Monomoy Island, and plunged into the storm, another call came over the radio from a Coast Guard cutter in the area, ten miles to the east. The cutter's captain was trying to ask the dragger captain how many crewmen he had aboard, but the draggerman's voice was answering, I assumed, in Portuguese. Then another voice came over the radio, a Portuguese one, from yet another dragger somewhere farther out to sea, and that voice succeeded in getting the voice from the *Doris L.* to speak English. The skipper of the *Doris L.* told the cutter captain that he had five aboard.

The three of us held on. We mashed through the toppling waves, gripping the bulkhead edge to keep from falling backward as we were rising, rising and rising as the big seas rushed under us, and then pressing against it as we hurtled down the face and plowed into the troughs.

Chuck had his hands full with the helm. When he looked up at the radar screen, his face went dull orange from the glow, and when he stared out through the windshield, his face was pale yellow from the compass light. Those lights, except for the cherry red numbers of the loran, the few gauges on the bulkhead, and our red and green running lights, were the only lights we could see.

Suddenly, we took one huge sea abeam that lifted the starboard side up so far, Chuck was holding on to the hauling door's handle as though it was over his head. All the drawers in the galley slid out and silverware smashed on the deck. Christo and I fell against the opposite side and something cracked—bone or wood, we weren't sure. The big tuna gaff with the ten-foot pole came loose from its rack and clattered across the deck.

"Shit," said Chuck when we had righted. I staggered aft to secure the tuna gaff under the net box aft, out of the way. We heard the wind screaming in the antennae. "Can't see the seas."

"You okay?" Christo asked, lighting a cigarette.

"Great," I said, planting my boots on the deck again and getting a firmer grip on the bulkhead. "Wonderful. Having fun." And all this was happening after two days at sea in dirty weather, catching nothing but cold and dogfish.

Radio confusion began again. The draggerman was yelling, "We need pump!" over and over, with the other Portuguese draggerman yelling back at him. An image of what was going on aboard the *Doris L.* flashed into my mind's eye: the men, in their oilskins, eyes wide and white, pupils pinpoints, their mouths dry, flailing madly with white plastic buckets at the sudsy water sloshing over their bunks, magazines and swollen paperbacks floating by them, the skipper at the helm with the radiophone in his fist, staring through the windshield at the rain and sleet, wondering why, why in the name of God he hadn't inspected the life raft in four years—now a useless rubber blanket lying at his feet.

"Mayday!" yelled the draggerman, followed the next moment by Chuck, peering into the radar screen, saying, "I think we have them." Christo and I, unintentionally holding on to each other as another heavy sea crashed over the bow, crowded around beside Chuck for a look.

"A mile, dead ahead," he said.

On the screen was one blip the size of a grain of rice. The sweep of the radar passed over it like a single spoke of a turning wheel. But at the hub of the sweep was a blossom of interference, sea clutter, and the blip was about to disappear into it.

Silent Lady took a horrendous, gut-dropping plunge and I squinched my eyes tight. The engine growled as we jolted on the bottom of the trough. Then we corkscrewed up through the other side of the wave and icy water jetted on my face from the windshield frame. Over the radio came the words, "Mayday, Mayday. Going down. Mayday."

The Coast Guard cutter started trying to raise the dragger and kept saying calmly, *"Doris L., Doris L. Come in Doris L."* I yanked a rag out of the lazaret, wiped my face, and stuffed the rag into the crack of the windshield frame.

Then Christo said, "What's that?"

"What's what?" I said. "What is it?"

"There," he said, pointing toward blackness. *"There they are!"*

Ahead, out of the blackness, a faint speck of white light was slashing back and forth. We bounded over a wave. The light vanished as we hit the trough, then reappeared when we crested the next wave.

Chuck got on the radio again to tell the *Doris L.* that we had sighted them. But the skipper must have panicked or his radio wasn't receiving, because all he said in reply was, "Mayday! Mayday!"

"You guys put your survival suits on," said Chuck.

"I thought they were for them," said Christo.

"Life jackets." was all Chuck said as we crept to the top of another wave and shot down its face.

I tussled with the zipper. I tugged at it, even put it between my molars and clamped down and wrenched at it with my jaw, but it wouldn't come free. I glanced up to see Christo sitting on the deck, jamming his legs into his suit. Stuck zipper or no stuck zipper, I was putting mine on. But I was in such a rush, I forgot to kick off my boots. I jammed my feet into the legs, anyway. Chuck, I knew, wouldn't put one on. He was of that school of fishermen that didn't know how to swim. If he found himself overboard, he would rather die quickly by drowning than drag things out by exposure.

My rubber boots got stuck against the rubber of the suit halfway down into the legs. The legs looked like two crimson snakes that had swallowed boots. The boat was heaving around. I was tossed from one side to the other. I pulled with all my might, but my boots wouldn't budge. I tried kicking them off, but that wouldn't work, either. I jumped up, standing there with the boots of the suit laid out in front of me as though my legs had broken at the calves and were folded at the wrong angle on the deck. I was just in time to see, through the windshield, a scene of such wildness and ferocity, I forgot that I was stuck half in and half out of my only means of survival should the *Silent Lady* also fall victim to the seas.

We were within thirty or forty yards of the *Doris L.* Chuck swung the searchlight on her. She was down by the stern. Her big flanged bow was jutting up toward the skies. It was strange, strange to see the palpable, real boat, the dark hull with the name *Doris L.* in white letters under her bow rail, the light at the masthead still burning bright, the white-green greedy seas diving one after the other onto her stern, the spindrift and sleet and rain and spray sizzling through the air, the wind shrieking. The voice still calling "Mayday! Mayday!" on the radio was unreal; now before us was a real boat, and real men with faces white as fish bellies standing along the forward rail, their orange and yellow and black oilskins glistening in the light. They waved at us insanely, almost like wild creatures. In the stark light of the searchlight that raked them as we dived and pitched through the seas, they jittered like figures in a nickelodeon, caught in another time, yards away from us but forever distant.

Now we were about fifty feet from them. We were going up and down on the waves like crazy, and the first time Christo heaved a line to them, it fell way short. The men on the rail were holding their arms out to us. Chuck maneuvered the *Silent Lady* a little closer, hesitant to get too close for fear that a big sea would shove us into her.

Christo was retrieving the line as fast as he could when one of the guys jumped into the water. The *Doris L.* was beginning to go down. Another jumped, and then another, like penguins plopping into a pool at the zoo, except here the water was wild. Soon they were all in the water, and since the radio had gone silent, we assumed that the skipper had jumped in, too.

"Throw them the life jackets!" yelled Chuck, and Christo and I grabbed them and flung them out like Frisbees. We got even closer, close enough to grab one of the fishermen and haul him up. We heaved him onto the deck and he vomited seawater. Christo tossed a line to another guy; he grabbed on and we hauled him hand over hand till we could hold him under the armpits and lift him aboard. We got another one, and another after that, and there was only one left, the skipper, I assumed, because the last one in the water was yelling at us in Portuguese in the same voice that had been yelling "Mayday."

Christo and I could barely lift our arms. My muscles quivered. In the water, the skipper clutched one of our life jackets and bobbed along until a big white comber rose up behind him and obliterated him.

We waited, all of us slamming around as the boat dived and jumped, trying to keep an eye on the sizzling white breaker that had wiped out the skipper. Then one of the survivors yelled, "There!"

He surfaced astern. One of the crewmen, Christo, and I, the survival suit still hobbling me, ran aft onto the open afterdeck. Christo tossed him another life jacket and a line. The skipper grabbed on and we hauled him up, almost surfing him along, we pulled so hard and fast. But we didn't have enough oomph to pull him all the way aboard over the gunwale.

I got up on the gunwale on my knees, the suit hanging below me. I felt him breathing, even felt his breath against my hands. He grinned up at me. I gripped his coat as if I was trying to rip it off him, yelling, "Now!" and we heaved again. The grinning skipper came popping up like a champagne cork, but there was just one problem.

I went in the other direction. With the final heave, a little pesky sea jolted the stern and I lost my balance. The skipper and I passed each other, he on his way to safety, me on my way into the drink. Still grinning, he looked at me with puzzlement in his eyes. As I went over, I saw that the *Doris L.* had been swamped and all that remained above the surface was the masthead light, still faithfully burning. Maybe the boat had already settled on the shoal. It couldn't have been very deep.

I was submerged into strange, humming silence.

I realized that I was looking at myself. It was as though I were seeing through the eyes of a fish, maybe a codfish or a pollock or a mackerel, or probably a dogfish. I saw myself there, hanging upside down, my arms flailing, my mouth agape, the survival suit's boots sticking up above the waves. I saw the white face, the bugged eyes, the gasping fish mouth with its ash white lips. The lips stretched, showing my white teeth. The eyes, bugging, turned to mine. A beam of white light began filtering down through the water, reaching like stilts and falling bright on Gordon's (mine!) ice white face and crimson survival suit. The column of light played over the upturned man, the beam probing downward into the depth until it could penetrate no more. Gordon was almost gone. His hands still reached toward the surface, upward, reaching for an invisible lifeline. The beam steadied, bathing him in the stark light, and then PAINPAINPAIN pain sucked the dogfish into the man, so that the man, the I, the dogfish fused with the drowning man, and I was I again, Gordon Holt, twenty-four, deckhand, overboard in a gale.

The pain was in my foot, my right foot. There was a nucleus of pain in the top of my foot, and the heat of this pain coursed outward in concentric circles. There was pressure with the pain, pressure that made my foot feel as though it were going to burst. Then there was tugging, tugging that twisted the pain. The water began to rush beside me, rush past my open eyes, seethe past me, tickle my face, and stream through my hair. I was pulled by the pain, propelled by it, and the pain yanked me free of the water, and I hit hard against something harder, and a roar was in my ears, and a sense of openness. No longer was my head enclosed in the helmet of the muffling sea. Voices and wind and the crash of waves and the growl of an engine were in my years, the open sound of the atmosphere, and icy air on my cheek, and the pain—oh, the pain was my foot. I hit something hard again, and I was on the boat, flat on my back on the deck.

"*E Jesus!*" said a Portuguese voice. Hands were all over me, crushing my ribs, and a warmth was on my mouth. I couldn't breathe! I couldn't breathe and I saw above me a man's face and the face came so close to mine that I lost the face, but I felt the warmth on my mouth. It happened again, and from around the face, rain and spray poured down onto my face. "*E Jesus!*" said the same voice. And then the seawater gushed out of me. I was coughing and gagging, and more seawater gushed out, and the mouth was on mine again. I felt the prickle of beard on my face, and I realized that I was breathing again. "You okay now," said the same voice. And there was the face, upside down over mine, grinning now, a swarthy face in stubble and seawater, the dragger skipper's face, the one I had passed on the way overboard. The deck was heaving. I dragged my fingers along it, feeling the cold, punky, soaked wood. Someone was tugging at my legs. I picked my head up off the deck to see Christo slicing away at my survival suit with a gutting knife. He smiled at me. The men from the *Doris L.* were hunkered around me, rain and spray dousing them. I eased my head back down on the deck.

"I catch you with gaff," yelled the dragger skipper. He grinned. Then a sear of pain made me jerk my head up, and at last I saw what caused it. The hook of the tuna gaff used for pulling in five-hundred-pound bluefin tuna was jammed through my boot. It went in at the top and reappeared out the other side, right through the sole of my boot.

"Leave it," yelled the skipper to Christo. "Keep from bleeding."

Then he looked at me, still upside down. He rested his hands on my shoulders and smiled. His teeth glowed against the sky. "You catch me, I catch you!" he said. "How much you think we bring at market?"

And I heard myself mumbling something, but what it was, I didn't know.

And he laughed hard, thumping my shoulders with his heavy hands. "Same price as dogfish!" he said. "Hey, but we, we *luckier!*" And he laughed harder, tipping his face up to the rain as we topped another wave and sliced down its homeward face.

CHILD IN THE
SHOALS

Andy Brown clung to the bell buoy. The buoy was never still, even when the sea lay flat calm. The tides and currents swept by it and rushed in a wake behind it as if it was making headway. The seaweed that had attached itself to the buoy streamed in the water. The buoy slowly undulated and spun on its chain. In a breeze, the waves broke constantly over the buoy. In a stronger wind, it pumped up and down, so that he had to grip with both hands on its steel tower. He felt like he was holding on to a carousel horse gone wild. He knew it was a miracle that he had been carried to the buoy in the first place. But the miracle was turning into damnation. It was like being marooned on a cork—only this cork was thirty miles from shore.

On the second day, he saw the bottom. It was a moon tide, the time of highest and lowest tides. The sandy shoals even this far from shore rose to nearly break the surface. In some spots during storms that struck at dead low tide, the water was so shallow, it was pulled away from the bottom in the trough of a huge breaker. Staring into the water, thinking of his wife, Kathy, and their two daughters, he knew that he could cling to the guano-encrusted buoy only until a big wave would wrench him off and he wouldn't have the strength to swim back and that would be the end. Then he was looking at sandy bottom with white seashells, as clear and close as if he had been swimming from the beach. But this bottom was thirty miles from any beach.

Swim for the bottom.

Other fishermen had said they would do it if they were ever shipwrecked, to save them the agony of dying by exposure or drowning. But had they ever been faced with it?

He had been faced with it. He was facing it. Maybe he should have done it the moment he hit the water, stroked down and down until his lungs filled with water and he stabilized and floated forever in Nantucket Shoals.

His lobster boat, the *Kathy Marie,* had been unceremoniously run down by a container ship that was twenty miles off its intended course in the shipping channel. The ship was fully loaded; containers were stacked ten-high fore and aft. Part of the reason the ship was so far away from where it should have been was that the helmsman wasn't at the helm. He was in the head, reading *People* magazine.

It was midday in a thick of fog. The 523-foot ship hadn't even slowed, probably hadn't even felt a hiccup as it mashed through the sixty-foot wooden boat. Aboard the *Kathy Marie,* Bobby Larsen, a crewman with only one other trip under his belt, had been on watch. Brown had gone aft to check on the load of new lobster traps they were going to set one hundred miles offshore. It was greasy calm, but the fog was so thick that he couldn't make out the bow of the *Kathy Marie* clearly from where he was working, aft on the stern. He realized now that he had had a false sense of security that arose from his decision to deliberately run so far inshore. He wanted to stay out of the zone of the big ships which he knew didn't keep close watch and which couldn't stop even if they were on a collision course. He had always been amazed at how quickly a small boat could get nearly nicked by a big one—even when the radar gave you fair warning. No, it was his fault: He shouldn't have gotten involved in the work. He should have kept checking the radar. The kid probably hadn't checked the radar the way he was supposed to. Of course, the container ship hadn't even been blowing its foghorn.

Brown had been clambering on the side of the traps that were stacked twelve-high in a ziggurat on the stern. He was at the top. He looked over his shoulder and saw the huge fluted bow above him and the Plimsoll line and the white waterline along the hull. He felt the *Kathy Marie* dip gently downward in the water that was being sucked underneath the bow wake of the container ship. He felt the vacuum in the air. He jumped instinctively when he saw the towering bow and the bow wake, hit the water, and was submerged. Underwater, he heard the thundering turbines. By the time he surfaced, spinning in a whirlpool in the stern wake left by the ship and its prop wash, he could see nothing but a circle of water around him. Some small pieces of lapstrake planking circled with him, along with a slowing sinking copy of *Playboy* and a crushed cereal box: the new box of cornflakes that had been among the groceries he had bought that morning before heading offshore.

Around that was fog.

He called for his crewmen, for Bobby Larsen. He called out for Dickie and Bert, both of whom had fished with him for nearly six years. They had been below in their bunks, reading, dozing, smoking, joking.

But there was no sound except for the calls of seabirds and his own splashes. As he kicked, he heard another sound: the bell buoy on the edge of Half Moon Shoal. It was still a few miles distant. He tried swimming for it, realizing that the fog would distort the sound. But he had no choice.

Then he touched a floating white object: a section of the *Kathy Marie*'s Styrofoam-insulated hold, enough for him to cling to.

He had not been a man who thought often about God, but he thanked him now. The section of hold was unstable and barely kept him above the water, but it was his world for the first few hours. He tried to steer the raft toward the sound of the bell buoy. He even heard the *thud thud thud* of a diesel engine—another fishing boat—heading offshore, somewhere in the fog. That same afternoon, another boat came so close, he heard a crewman talking. He heard the voice say, so casually, so carelessly (but how would the crewman know that as he cruised along at twelve knots, not fifty feet from the hull of his boat, a man was clinging to a piece of wreckage?), after a brief laugh, "The big one? Or the little one?"

It came to Brown from the fog like a ghost's voice. Brown knew even if he yelled, the crewman would not hear him over the sound of the diesel. Or, if he did, the crewman would wonder what he had heard, and by then it would be too late, the boat would have passed out of range.

But Brown yelled out in spite of himself, one long, rising "Hey" that was swallowed the minute it left his tongue. The thud of the engine receded. He wished he hadn't called out. He kicked the water, tensed against the panic ringing in his ears.

When the sound of the boat had nearly vanished, there was a new sound that made him paddle faster: He thought some large sea creature was skimming along the surface for him. But it was the wake of the boat that had passed by so close, sizzling toward him. It swept over him and onward and disappeared into the fog. Then all was silent again.

It was maddening trying to find the bell buoy. The bell kept gonging but never seemed to get closer. It was the number-five bell buoy, the one on the edge of Half Moon Shoal he had passed so many times going to and from the fishing grounds. It had become less of a marker than a shadow in his unconscious. The only way he would have noticed it was if it wasn't there. But now it was everything.

Finally, he began paddling in a pattern, taking ten strokes in one direction crosscurrent and stopping to listen. In this way he eventually came upon the buoy, minutes before total darkness had set in. The buoy loomed up much larger and sounded much louder than he had imagined, everything magnified by the fog—or distorted, since to see anything, you had to be within a few feet of it. In his scramble from the raft to the buoy, the raft sank down a few inches, then lolled over and settled with only one corner protruding from the green water, iceberglike. In the morning it would be gone.

And so began his long wait. His first item of business was to silence the clapper on the bell. The clapper was as big as a sledgehammer. He ripped off a trouser leg and lashed the clapper to one of the buoy's struts. He would have been deaf and insane in half a day had he not stopped the random clanging that could be heard five miles away and even farther from a vessel under sail. In his climb up to the buoy, he had lacerated himself on the barnacles and bled as if from a hundred paper cuts.

The fog stayed with him for the first two days. Every morning, the Concorde leaving from New York City jolted him with its sonic boom as it accelerated toward Europe.

Below, on the surface of the Atlantic Ocean, Brown licked from the struts of the buoy the fresh water of the dew that formed in the fog. He realized that New York City and Europe and airplanes were from a different planet than the one he inhabited. He licked the water that beaded up on his forearms, and the water he wrung from his flannel shirt. By then the Concorde was beyond the curve of the earth.

He listened to seabirds. Gulls tried to land but flew off when they saw him. He listened to waves. Large ones sounded like huge plastic bags shaking in a high wind as they broke past him.

Once, a school of porpoises exploded by. One of them circled, blowing water out of its blowhole, shaking its head and eyeing him as if imploring him to join their merry band. Then it flipped beads of water from its glistening back and jetted off with one muscular push of its tail.

That night the sky cleared and thousands of stars twinkled right down to the horizon in every direction. It was that night that Brown made out the tiny fan of light beyond the horizon. The light was cast by the island of Nantucket, a place with people on another planet thirty light-years away, as remote as Vega, Sirius, Aldebaran, Bellatrix, or Arcturus.

After the third day his mind and eyes began playing tricks on him. In the mornings he saw the Concorde's contrail and the jet seemed to be moving so fast and so straight that it shot overhead in two seconds. He lay panting after the plane was gone, watching the contrail drift quickly to the south.

He wouldn't have lasted a day or even five minutes in the water had it been anything other than early August, when the surface water was fifty-eight degrees, as warm as it would get all year. But together, the sea, sky, wind, and sun were working away at him.

At night he could see the lights of the draggers towing their nets, working back and forth, five miles, ten miles, sometimes within a mile of him, so close that he could see figures moving about under the deck lights.

One beautiful morning, he watched a dragger appear on the horizon and steam toward him. *God, oh God!* he thought. *This is it!* At about a thousand yards, the boat slowed to an idle. He was saved! Thank God, he was saved! She idled over to him and then hove to at about twenty feet. She was a tumbledown old bucket with a list to port and rust streaks from the scuppers and rusty rigging and a sweet smell of decaying fish and a pile of old torn net on her afterdeck. No one came out on deck even though it was a brilliantly sunny day, the swells were high but easy, and the water sparkled with jewels. For nearly a half hour, the boat wallowed within ten feet of him, her seaworn rigging swaying, pumping some foul liquid out of her bilge that brought blue sharks up from the depths. Brown waved and waved, screaming, "Help! Help me!" over and over. Wasn't that someone inside there, in the pilot-house? That was someone for certain! "Hey you—you at the helm! I'm here! Come out! Hey! Help! What the hell is the matter? *Save me!*"

But then the boat's engine revved up. A column of black smoke spewed from the stack. She sidled off, swinging her stern to him and heading out to sea, toward the same horizon she had appeared from. He watched the boat go over one swell, disappear into the trough, then reappear to angle up over the face of another swell, disappear, reappear on a distant swell, crest it, and then disappear altogether.

He clenched his hands around the huge bolts on the buoy and looked into the blue sky and prayed to hold on, to his buoy, to his mind.

On the afternoon of the fourth day, he had been watching the horizon and seeing only seabirds when he blinked and blinked again and then saw little children walking toward him across the water. He recognized two of them, his own children, Amy and Lynn, ages five and seven. Behind them and fanned out to either side were many other children he didn't know. They all looked intent, very serious. They moved toward him cautiously. All had their eyes on him. There were many children moving toward him in a ragtag broken line, maybe a hundred, perhaps a thousand. From one horizon to another, he saw nothing but children, like a migration, or the vanguard of the Children's Crusade. There was golden light coming from a lowering sun. A breeze moved through the children's hair. He saw Amy's dirty blond hair fluttering, and she made that happily exasperated grin as she swiped her unruly hair away from her face. Lynn's hair was also fluttering, but it was darker, befitting her serious nature, and it flowed gracefully away from her oval face. The line of children swept by him like a slow wave. As they passed, the children kept their eyes on him. Lynn looked at him with her large clear brown eyes and jet black pupils that Andy Brown so loved to gaze into and she said, "Come with us, Daddy. We're going home," but before he could answer, the line of children was beyond him across the cobalt waves and vanished over the horizon to blend into the whitecaps.

He could no longer feel his hands gripping the big bolts or the iron struts of the buoy. He stared over his shoulder at the whitecaps for a long time. There was nothing out there; he moved his head to a more comfortable position, and the same whitecaps appeared to lie in that direction.

In the distance, he saw a few seabirds flapping in the sky. Gannets? Shearwaters? Gulls? Arctic terns? His eyes were playing tricks on him. One moment, he was seeing children and the next he was seeing open ocean. He hoped that the seabirds would not come his way. But more and more often, they landed on the buoy. His skin was crackled and blistered by the sun and the wind like a baked chicken. In other spots, it was pickled, peeling away from his hands and face from exposure to the salt water.

The seabirds began to get used to him and reclaimed their old roost. Gulls perched on the top of the tower and gazed seaward, aloof, ignoring him. He had tried to eat their excrement but it filled his mouth with chalk. To save energy he lay belly-down on the buoy, the surge of the swells washing over him. Lying belly-down protected his face from the sun, but his neck became blistered. He had little to worry about from the birds, except getting shit on. The birds were after a place to rest. Still, one blood-eyed gull had pecked at him, testing him to see whether he was alive.

There had been one blind gannet that had stayed with him for two days. By finding the buoy, the big bird had finally lucked on something solid to alight on. Brown thought the gannet was much like himself—this in spite of the fact that Brown tried to capture and eat the bird. Gannets dive-bombed schools of fish from tremendous heights; over the course of a lifetime of these diving and feeding frenzies, the shock of hitting the water sometimes blinded them. They had no natural protection for their eyes, except for a black band of feathers that made them look like bandits and perhaps helped cut the sea glare.

He grabbed at it to kill it and eat it, but the bird was tough and nimble and slashed him with its beak. It flew off but then circled back and landed again.

This gannet, its big beak cracked and yellow, stayed with him and caught sand eels and a few hake that passed the buoy. It treated Brown as if he were a young gannet and tried to feed him. At first he thought the bird was trying to attack. But the gannet, its deep eye sockets containing lightless soft beads, put first one little fish on his shoulder, then one on his head, then a mass of them in his hand, apparently aiming for but not finding his mouth. This was what saved the bird. Otherwise Brown would have tried again and again to wring its neck and eat it. But now he was being fed. Other birds, gulls mostly, pestered them, hoping for tidbits. They flapped like white windblown litter around them, their shadows crisscrossing the thick, chipped, water-splashed red paint of the buoy.

The bird stayed for two days. Then one morning before light, Brown heard a flap and a rustle. When daylight came, the bird was gone.

As the sun rose higher, a Coast Guard search plane, a Hercules, orange and white and roaring, circled five miles to the east, its wings glinting in the sunlight. It circled for what seemed like the entire morning. Then it straightened out and flew fast to the northwest.

That was when the porpoises returned. It seemed to Brown that the same one who had looked at him before this time poked its head out of the water and said, "Don't worry, the children will be back."

Then the porpoises were gone. Brown was so grateful for having heard a human voice that he thought nothing of the fact that a porpoise had spoken to him.

The seabirds called and toward dusk flew shoreward in loose formations, their day done. After a red-and-purple-and-peach sunset, night came on and the stars shined out and a wind sprang up.

Some time in the night, as Brown was shivering and watching shooting stars drop out of the sky, keeping his back to the faint fan of light beyond the horizon that was Nantucket, which glowed like a distant and unattainable carnival, at some time in the night, there was a voice next to him.

"Hi, Daddy," it said. The voice was a child's voice, a little girl's.

"Hello," said Brown. "Is that you, Amy?"

"Uh-huh."

"Amy, honey. How's your sister? How's your mother?"

"They told me to come out here to . . . ummm . . ."

"Why, honey? Can you remember why they told you to come out here?"

"I don't know."

"Try, honey. Try to remember."

"Umm. They . . . told . . . me . . . to . . ."

"Go on."

"They told me to . . . to tell you that . . ."

"You can remember, honey."

"Umm. They told me to tell you that . . ."

"Go on."

And the voice giggled triumphantly.

"I remember! They told me to tell you *to come home safe!*"

Out of the dark, a big wave washed over Brown so that he sputtered and spat seawater. He held on tightly to the buoy. Night was the worst because the only way to tell if a wave was approaching was by its phosphorescent crest. But even then depth perception was a problem and the waves would approach cloaked in darkness and crash over him before he could prepare himself.

"Amy?" he yelled into the night. "Amy? Amy, where are you?"

Panic overswept him as he thought that the wave had washed his daughter off the buoy.

"A-A-M-E-E-E-E!" he screamed to the stars and the waves, and then he knew he had to go in after her, to save her, to save his daughter.

Diving into the water felt cleansing and purifying. Maybe it was immersion in the cold salt water that laved his sun-scorched, barnacle-sliced skin and stanched the stinging pain of his open sores and cracked lips and suffering mind. Instead of being wracked by many elements, he was now in one. He had chosen one. He angled his body downward, kicked and stroked underwater, all the time feeling ahead of him in the dark water for his daughter. He swam downward and away from the buoy, now forgetting it and its tortures. He wanted to call out for his Amy; he wanted to search her out and pull her to safety, save her life!

He touched bottom and ran his hand along the silky sand, here in this spot fifteen feet underwater, thirty miles offshore, a spot of sand never before having been touched by a human.

Still he did not rise, but swam for his lost daughter, his child lost in the shoals.

HARWICH PORT

It's two-thirty in the morning. A mist sweeps across the deck lights as we unload hundred-pound boxes of codfish from the boat onto the truck up on the pier. It's low tide, and the boat is six feet below the level of the pier, so we have to slip each box into a rope sling attached to a boom on the back of the truck. The codfish are covered in ice, curled, their fins stiff. My toes, even in my fishing boots, feel colder.

"Berk's making the next trip," says Ted, the skipper, his breath blowing along with the mist. "Stop down in the morning for your pay."

"No problem," I say, pulling up one last fish from the ice at the bottom of the hold and tossing it into a box. "Can you give me a lift home tonight?"

"Maybe Pete can."

Once we've unloaded the catch and washed down the *Shirley B.,* I ask Pete, the other crewman, to take me to my girlfriend's house. He drops me at the end of the drive. The drive is icy at the edges. The house is black. I tap at the door, once, twice, three times. I'm shivering out in the mist and the cold. The only noise is the wind in the trees.

My seabag is getting soggier and heavier with the wet.

The door creaks open.

"It's me," I whisper.

"You stink," she says.

"I'm freezing." I stamp my boots.

"Take your boots off."

The door opens and I shoulder in, leaving my seabag and boots in the vestibule. She takes my hand and leads me through the black house, up steep stairs to her room, where she has an old bed with a mattress that once belonged to her grandfather, a mattress that's stuffed with corn shucks. She has a ton of quilts, blankets, and comforters on the bed. I steal into the bathroom, cat-wash, feel my way back to the room, and ease underneath the pile of covers, crackling the corn shucks. I crush my girlfriend's bed-hot body to the length of my body and hold on tightly.

My girlfriend rises before five to go to work, but we make love quickly before she showers. I don't even get to linger in bed or take a scalding shower; her father doesn't like me in the house when she's not there. She gives me a lift back down to the harbor; I don't want to miss getting paid, and if I go home, I might sleep too long. We part and I walk down the dark pier. The mist still blows. I'm dog-tired. I know Ted keeps the key to the pilothouse door on top of the afterdeck light, and so I go inside out of the mist and cold. I kick off my boots and dig out a pair of sneakers from my seabag. Then I sit on the deck under the helm and wait.

At ten, Ted jumps aboard, and I wake up with a jolt. I'm sprawled on the deck. I get up, stiff and dizzy. The pilothouse is cold but dry. The mist is sweeping across the harbor and the pines around the edge are boxing with the wind. Berk hasn't arrived yet.

"If he doesn't show, I'm available," I say, counting the cash Ted has counted out to me: two hundred dollars for three days of gillnetting in dirty weather. Ted puts his newspaper on the bulkhead and rips a smile out of the cover of his coffee cup. The windshield is bleary with mist. He says, "Thanks, we'll see," and flips the page of his newspaper. I take my orange Helly-Hansen oilskin overalls and jacket off the hook. They're splotched with dried fish blood, but I fold them up carefully and pack them in my seabag.

As I hop off the boat on to the pier, I see Chuck getting aboard the *Big Blue,* a lobster boat.

"Hey Chuck!" I call. "You need crew?" I toss my seabag on the pier and trot over, my hands thrust into my plaid wool jacket pockets. Mist beads up on the fibers. I squint against the mist. My toes are freezing through my sneakers. I pull up the hood of the gray sweatshirt that I'm wearing underneath my jacket.

"Not this trip," he says, standing on the rail. "But Kevin's taking a trip off around Thanksgiving."

"Count me in."

"Yeah. We'll see."

"How've you been doing?"

"Terrible. Worst I've seen in years."

"Well, see you later."

"Later."

I hitch home. My place is off a dead-end sand lane in pine woods. It's a one-room apartment off a winterized cottage. The couple that rents the main part of the house has a two-year-old boy who wakes up in the middle of the night screaming. The father is a welder; she's a nurse. He hasn't pulled his truck out of the driveway since I moved in last year, after I dropped out of college and came home to Harwich Port. When the boy wakes up, they yell at him, "Shut up!" Usually after he quiets down, they start fighting.

I don't have a telephone. I don't want the bother, and the down payment seems like extortion. The fridge that came with the place is like the one in my college dormitory, only it has less mold. My built-in electric heater heats an area only directly in front of it.

I turn it on full blast and stand barefoot as close to it on the linoleum floor as I can. Then I strip and get in the shower. Soon the hot water peters out; the couple and I share a hot-water heater. The out-of-work welder spends his mornings in the shower. Still, I manage to get clean. My toes and fingers are permanently wrinkled, as though I'd fallen asleep in the bathtub. Now I must either sleep or take my dirty clothes to the laundromat. I'm so tired, I could lean against the wall and fall asleep, like a horse. But if I don't wash my clothes, and if I get a slot on a boat this afternoon or tomorrow, I'll be forced to wear wet, reeking jeans, long johns, shirts, and socks. So I pack my seabag with laundry, put on my warm parka and dry work boots, and head out beneath the dripping pines. I walk up the sand road to the beach road and then the mile to the main road. Two cars pass. Then Chuck's pickup approaches, going in the wrong direction, and he honks as he passes by. I would have ridden the bike that I keep behind my place (actually it's my girlfriend's), but I thought I wouldn't be able to balance the huge bag of laundry and ride at the same time. Now, standing in the cold mist by the road, I wish I'd tried.

By 3:30, I'm heading back from the laundromat. I pass Bank Street and debate whether or not to stop in to see Mom. I decide not to; she'll want me to fix something, and I've got to stop by the harbor to see what's up. It's already getting dark when I get there. No one is around. Boats rock in their slips. The mist swirls down. Outside lights from the boat-works buildings glitter on the waves in the harbor. Gulls stand around on top of pilings and cabintops, looking miffed. I lug my laundry back up to the main road and walk most of the way home before getting a lift from an old man for the last quarter mile. I conk out for a few hours on my bed, then take a hot shower. I decide to head back into town on my bike for a few beers at The Landing.

I'm soaked by the time I get there. Remmick and Tracy are at the bar, already drunk. They're in a lip-lock. They look like they've got an extra set of arms each. They unlock long enough for Remmick, his curly blond hair all mussed by Tracy's hands, to look at me with hooded eyes and say, "Nasty out." Tracy doesn't even look at me. Then they go back to kissing.

I order a beer from Ken, the bartender, a guy I went to high school with who spent a few years in the Coast Guard, and then I go to the phone in the entrance hall to call my girlfriend.

"Come on down. I'll buy you a drink," I say.

"Okay."

I wait for her at the bar. Remmick says, "I haven't been out for a week." He can afford it because he makes most of his money selling anything illegal he can lay his hands on. But he's still a smart fisherman. I finish my first beer and order a second when in walks Berk.

"How's the hand?" I say.

"Still hurts like fucking hell," he says. He orders a beer and sits on a stool beside me. He's a long, tall, dark-haired guy with a ponytail and a nose broken in a zigzag. He grins a lot and laughs a lot and his lips always seem wet. "Take a look," he says, unwrapping an Ace bandage from his right hand.

He uncovers a grotesque bloated thumb with skin that's peeling off it. "Doctor up there says I should be happy the nail's all I'll lose. Gave me a shot of penicillin in the ass that hurt worse than my thumb. When he dug the spine out, you should have seen the pus fly."

"You making the next trip?" I ask.

"Got to."

We drink our beers and give each other a look when Remmick gets up to go the bathroom, leaving Tracy to straighten herself out. She crosses her legs, smooths her short skirt, and tugs at her stockings. She bounces a leg and dangles a high heel and looks at us as though we're two sections of the same wall.

My girlfriend arrives and we move to a table. She tells me her father is going out to his regular bridge party at Mrs. Currier's for the evening. After a couple of drinks, we leave to go to her house. I throw my bike into the back of her old salt-rotted Volvo station wagon. Spending an evening together is rare, since when I'm ashore, she still has to get up so early to go to the fish market. Even rarer is spending an evening in her house without her father glaring at me over his pipe. It's a good thing the pipe smoking killed his sense of smell, or he'd sniff me out when I sneak in after a trip offshore.

We go up the steep stairs to her room. Sinking to the middle of the bed, we make love, the bed crackling beneath us, but we haven't had time to finish before we hear a car come in the driveway and the front door open and close.

"Damn it," she says. "Mrs. Currier probably passed out too early."

"I'll go out the back," I say. There's an old wooden back stairway off her father's room that looks like it might fly away in the next strong blow.

"No, stay. Just be quiet and I'll tell him I'm feeling lousy and going to bed early."

"Okay."

In the early-morning darkness, we steal downstairs and she drives me home. I get the bike out of the back and kiss her good-bye. On the floor under my front door is a piece of paper.

"Couldn't find you. Frank" is all it says.

"Shit," I say as the taillights of my girlfriend's car disappear up the sand road. "Shit, shit, shit."

I pedal back up the road and most of the way to the harbor. When I'm more than halfway there, Chuck passes, then stops and picks me up. I put the bike in the back of his pickup.

"Frank was looking for you," he says. "Sorry I couldn't give you a lift the other day. I had to get to the bank about the boat mortgage."

"That's okay. I can't believe I missed Frank."

Chuck drags on his cigarette and shifts the gears.

We get to the harbor as the sky is lightening, but Frank's boat is already out of its slip.

"Oh well," says Chuck. "What can you do?"

I walk with him down to *Big Blue.*

"You guys heading out?" I say.

"Bilge pump shit the bed, but after I fix it, we're heading out."

"Well, good luck."

"See you at the end of the week."

I pedal into town to Ike's for breakfast. The weather hasn't changed, except the wind has lightened. The carpenters and roofers and plumbers are eating eggs and drinking coffee and smoking cigarettes and reading papers. I sit next to John Sears, the harbormaster.

"If you're looking for some work, I've got some that pays fifty bucks." He says the Town of Harwich wants to clean one of its rivers of brush and deadfall that clogged it up during the last storm. The herring swim upstream in the spring and need clear sailing. We finish breakfast and he takes me up to the headwaters of the river, near where the herring run is.

"Just work your way down and clean out all the crap till you reach the first bridge. That's where I'll meet you." He lets me borrow his waders and he gives me a small ax and a handsaw. I spend the day wading in belly button–high water, hauling out snags, cutting fallen trees.

When I reach the first bridge, he isn't there. I sit and watch the tide rise in the river. The sky is clearing; soft pinks and blues appear in the sky where the sun has set, and the mist draws away from the marsh.

"Sorry," he says when he finally pulls up. "Coughlin lost his stuffing box and he was sinking at the gas dock. We had to pump him out. Here's your fifty bucks."

He gives me a lift down to the harbor so I can wait for Frank. I take my bike out of the back of his pickup. Whenever I start off with the bike, I get rides. Whenever I don't have it, I don't.

Berk and Pete are working on gear on the afterdeck of the *Shirley B.*

"You guys heading out?" I say.

"If the weather holds," says Pete.

"How's your thumb?"

Berk grins and holds up an Ace-bandaged thumb wrapped in plastic.

"That'll last a few more minutes," I say. "Heard anything from Frank?"

"They were on the radio a while back. Sounds like they're down around Nantucket."

"Probably hauling the last of his fish traps."

Ted backs down the pier in his pickup and Pete and Berk help him unload groceries.

"About the only thing you can say for the fucking cold is that you don't need to buy ice," Ted says to me.

"You said it," I say. "Cold's here to stay. Good luck, you guys."

"See you in a day or two."

I help them cast off and then I walk back up to the phone at the end of the pier. The *Shirley B.* is making the turn to head into the outer harbor, leaving a ribboning wake in the last light, as I reach my girlfriend at work.

"When you getting off?"

"We're doing inventory. Counting every lobster in the place. Probably not until eight."

"How about dinner at The Landing?"

"Sure."

It's nearly eight by the time Frank's boat makes the inner harbor.

"Where you been, boy?" says Frank as he tightens the spring line. "Upstream spawnin'?" he says with a grin. He has plenty of teeth, but they all seem to have wide spaces between them. His glasses are salt-speckled.

His son, Frank Junior, has already unloaded three boxes loaded with lobsters from the boat. I help him heft another four boxes onto the pier. He doesn't say "Thanks" or even "Get out of my way" to me as he goes up to the parking lot and backs the pickup down the pier, screaming the truck backward at top speed. He's never had a word—let alone a kind one—for anyone.

"Lucked out with lobsters today," says Frank, still on the boat. "I wanted to go offshore to pick up some gear that got torn up in the storm, but I couldn't find crew, so we stayed inshore to pull our fish traps. Got a nice surprise. I said to Junior, 'Hell, let's let the goddamn gear soak another week.' Now where you think all these fucking bugs are coming from? Haven't seen any inshore since Teddy and I slayed them in the late fifties. You up for a trip to the Canyons to haul gear tomorrow?"

I say sure. He tells me to be aboard at five; he'll give me $150 flat.

"Sorry you missed a payday today, boy," he says. "But you got laid, didn't you?"

I smile.

"Hell, boy, you're the one who made out—what am I goddamn apologizin' for?"

He gets off the boat with a groan and climbs in the passenger side of the pickup truck. His son squeals the tires, leaving the stink of rubber on the pier. I pedal down to The Landing, where my girlfriend is already waiting.

"I feel like getting drunk," she says. "If I close my eyes, all I see is lobsters." She hoists her beer and finishes it.

"I'm going offshore tomorrow," I say.

"For how long?"

"Probably just an overnight."

"Order me a beer."

We drink for a while and then order cheeseburgers.

"Let's stay at my place tonight," I say. "Leave your father to himself."

"I'm not done drinking yet," she says, her cheeks red.

"Me either."

We drink more. Remmick and Tracy come in and sit at our table. They begin talking at us rapid-fire, drinking brandy almost as fast as they talk. I catch my girlfriend's eye and roll my eyes. Soon Remmick and Tracy get up to leave.

"I'm heading offshore jigging tomorrow, if you're interested," he says. "I hear they're on the move early."

"How far you going?"

"To the Channel."

"I'm supposed to go haul gear with Frank tomorrow."

"Where're you going?"

"The Canyons. He said he's got gear torn up from the last storm."

"He paying you a share?"

"Flat fee."

"You come with me, I'll pay you a full share."

"I don't know. I can't let Frank down."

"No, you can't at that. Some other time."

★ ★ ★

After last call, we get in the Volvo. I drive. We weave down the empty roads to my place. We try to make love in the cold room. My girlfriend shivers. As we begin to warm up, the little boy in the main house begins screaming and my girlfriend says, "What do they do, stick him with hot needles?" She lies back and pulls the covers over her head and eventually passes out, breathing beer fumes on me. I stay awake, alternately sweating and shivering, listening to my neighbors fight. The alarm goes off at 4:45, the very second, it seems, that I finally fall asleep. It takes me nearly ten minutes to wake up my girlfriend and then she uses all the hot water in the shower.

As we head out into the dark morning, crows in the pines begin yelling.

"Shut up," whispers my girlfriend. "Tell them to shut up."

"I'm sick," she says as I drive her to work.

"You're hung over," I say. I look at her slumped in her parka against the door, her blond hair mashed against the window.

She mumbles, "I wish I could die."

Still bleary and half-drunk after I drop her and her car off at the market, I walk the three miles to Ike's and eat a breakfast of three poached eggs on toast, home fries, bacon, sausage, a side of raisin toast, a corn muffin, coffee, orange juice, and milk. I read the paper and everything in it irritates me. I leave and walk homeward, the day dawning clear, cold, and windless—a perfect day to head offshore. As I walk, I calculate. With the 150 bucks from Frank, I can pay my rent. It's only seventy-five bucks a month, but that's a lot for what I get. I can buy groceries. Maybe save for a down payment on a phone and an answering machine, so I won't miss jobs. And toward the end of the month, if I work for Chuck, that could be a good-sized paycheck. If only I could get a regular slot. Soon the dead of winter will be here and I'll have to scrape around for work or head down to the Keys to crew. I don't want to spend

the winter shucking sea scallops or plowing snow with Dick. But I
don't have enough money to make it down to the Keys.

I fall on my unmade bed and sleep until noon. I wake up in
the same position, feeling better. I shave and pack my seabag and
head off for the pier, where I'll drop my bag, and then town, where
I'll eat again. As I walk, I notice that some mare's tails are forming
in the sky to the west, which might or might not mean a change in
the weather.

All the boats are out except for Frank's. After dropping my
bag off at the boat, I go to The Landing. Ken gives me my first beer
free, " 'Cause I feel like it," he says. A free beer at a bar always tastes
better.

I call my girlfriend and insist that she come for lunch.

"Eating's the only thing that'll help you recover," I say.

"Dying's the only thing."

She arrives and I buy her a Bloody Mary and a cheeseburger.

"I know you," she says. "You're the one who got me into
trouble last night."

My grilled ham-and-cheese sandwich arrives. "I'd do it again
tonight, but I've got to go offshore," I say.

By the time we finish lunch, it's after three. My girlfriend
takes me to the harbor and then heads back to work. Frank and his
son are already aboard. They're standing in the pilothouse, listening
to the weather on the radio. When I come in, Frank Junior turns
and says, "What's a college kid like you doing this kind of work for,
anyway?"

I say I'm not a college kid. He laughs and pushes by me and
walks off the boat and onto the pier.

Frank says, "Don't mind him. Money's eating him. He's
heading out to Colorado Saturday to plow for the ski areas and he
doesn't have a pot to piss in because he drank up all his money. He's
got worries."

We stand listening to the weather. It sounds bad. I think, *If*

Frank Junior's leaving Saturday, what day is today? And what's tomorrow?

The weather report says it's Tuesday. That's what going offshore does to you. Tides matter. Barometric pressure matters. Moons matter. It's easy to lose track of the days of the week. There are no weekends, no quitting times.

"Breeze of wind coming, boy. Nothing we can do. Check back at the boat tomorrow. Least I can do is give you some shore work, stacking traps, whatever."

What I'm interested in is going offshore, not shore work. But I've got bills to pay. "All right, Frank," I say. "Need any help now? I'm not doing squat."

I end up helping Frank Junior change the engine oil. Down in the bilge, his hands black, his knuckles bleeding, he says, "My old man drives me bugfuck."

By the time we're done, Remmick's boat comes in the harbor.

"Jesus, did we hit them," he says. He got Berk's cousin Mike to go with him, a green hand. "But we got beat up pretty bad."

"How much?" says Frank, looking down into the fish box of Dick's boat from the pier.

"About four thousand pounds," says Dick. "Almost all steaker cod."

"That's a day's pay," says Frank. "Where'd you hit them?"

"The Crushed Shells."

He nods as though he knew it all along.

I look at all the codfish lying in the fishbox. I reach into the pocket of my jeans and finger the rest of my slim wad of cash.

That night, the big blow reaches shore. A low has intensified off Nova Scotia and spreads southeast, a rare occurrence. The *Shirley B.* runs back in before the storm with seven thousand pounds of codfish. The *Big Blue* makes it back in from the Northern Edge with a small load of lobsters. All the other boats make it back in before the storm. Forty-foot seas are reported offshore on Georges Bank. Later, at high tide, the pier is overwhelmed by waves, and a few shanties, where the fishermen stow their gear, are washed above the road into a field. Most of the beach along Nantucket Sound is washed away. All the work I'd done clearing out the river is undone as a tidal surge swamps it and pushes all the deadfall back. In town, the A&P, fearing floods, runs out of sandbags and stacks bags of Kitty Litter out front instead.

My girlfriend's father has gone to play bridge at Mrs. Currier's again; we decide to drink at The Landing for a while. We sit at a table and listen to Berk and Pete and Chuck and Remmick tell about the house-high waves they ran from. I tell them about the time Remmick and I almost capsized off Monomoy Point in a gale at daybreak.

"Yeah, I almost shit my drawers when that happened," he says. "I was looking down at you, and behind you was nothing but green water. But you should have gone with me this time." He drinks from his beer mug, then sets the mug down. "After this blow, the fishing'll be all fucked up."

"I know," I say. "But Frank'll come through."

Later, my girlfriend and I head to her house. Her father calls to say that Deep Hole Road is flooded and that he can't make it back that night.

"He must be playing strip bridge with Mrs. Currier," she says.

We take our time on the crunchy mattress.

Branches tick at the window and the wind hits the house with hard hollow-sounding gusts. My girlfriend turns onto her stomach and falls asleep, her arm across my chest. I run my hand over her hip and the curve of her thigh, but she doesn't wake up. I pull the covers over us. I hear creaks and groans coming from outside. I wonder if the stairway off her father's room is working loose, hanging on by a rusty nail or two. I lie there on my back a long time, listening to the weather and my girlfriend's breathing, thinking of house-high waves and unpaid bills.

And I wonder, *What's tomorrow? What day of the week is it today, and what will it be tomorrow?*

A SAILOR'S
VALENTINE

The memory of her lips hot against his made him momentarily forget that he was straining to haul seventy pounds of heaving codfish by hand from a depth of sixty fathoms. He saw her before him, slight, small, pressing her body against his. And then he groaned twice, once from the memory of the kiss on the dock the night before he left on this trip offshore, the second time at the reality of where he was: sixty miles offshore in the Atlantic Ocean, hauling a fighting weight as fast as he could with taut cod line cutting through his wet cotton gloves. This was what it had been like ever since they'd met two weeks before: sudden vivid memories of his moments with her that made him stand stock-still and stare at the horizon without realizing he was doing so. They were like petit mal fits of love.

Ford stopped hauling and glanced at his mate, who continued hauling line as fast as he could on the afterdeck. Seeing Arnie work so hard, tiny bullets of salt water zinging off the line into the sunshine as the line ascended, the tensed line sending out shivers on the smooth green surface of the water, his bearded chin jutted out at the horizon and his eyes blank from fatigue, all of it made Ford resentful. He felt as though Arnie was the sole reason he had to go nearly a hundred miles offshore day in and day out, when if Arnie had said he wanted to take a day off, Ford could stay ashore and spend time with Sue. Never mind that it was the best fishing of the season and that what they made during this time of the summer when the codfish schooled up carried them through the rest of the year. No, Arnie didn't know the first thing about love, Ford decided, and he wouldn't have understood even if he yelled to him for a year over the mumbling diesel engine.

Ford thought that Mike, his black-and-white mutt, who was watching him from his perch on the engine cover, knew more about love than Arnie did. Being mean to Arnie for a moment made him feel better, then a trickle of guilt like acid burned him and he felt terrible for turning on Arnie, who was as trustworthy as they came. His aimless thoughts were interrupted as the end of his line neared and three heavy fish appeared from green depths, their bellies snow white. Ford gaffed them and hefted them each aboard in turn.

The fish kept biting. Under high blue skies, they hauled until slack tide. Shearwaters and fulmars and petrels and gulls bobbed and flapped around the boat, awaiting morsels. Then the fish let up and Ford suggested that they run for home, that they probably had three thousand pounds of fish aboard. But Arnie looked at him cockeyed and said, "Maybe a thousand," so they drifted back over the spot. Ford felt a mixture of embarrassment and resentment at Arnie having called his bluff. Why wouldn't he play along? He went back to hauling with a kind of vengeance.

Normally Ford would have realized that the fishing never got any better than this. The tides were weak so their jigging lines didn't get swept up to nearly float on the surface 360 feet away, as happened so often when the tide ran hard. No other boats were in the vicinity to bother them, especially the gill-netters that would set nets directly on a school or the draggers that would steam over a spot and scoop up every fish. The wind was calm, the seas were flat as sheet metal, the sun was shining, and all they wore were T-shirts, oilskin overalls, rubber boots, and cotton gloves. Their faces and forearms got sunburned. They were catching huge steaker codfish, so that between the two of them, they boated nearly two hundred pounds of fish each haul. They were in a dead haul, where each time they threw the jigs back over, they hooked up fish.

But he wanted to scream, he wanted so badly to be back with Sue. He wanted to feel her slight body against his, touch her glossy black hair with its undertones of henna, listen to her voice, her breathing, look into those rich chestnut eyes, brush that stone-smooth skin. But it was more than that. He looked across the miles of shining water to the horizon, the frontier between them, and thought how long it was going to take before the day was over, how long even after the day was over it would take to steam back home over the sea beyond that horizon.

The fishing flagged during the early afternoon. Then, just after three o'clock, the fish stopped biting altogether. Ford said they'd better get headed home or they wouldn't be able to make the market. When Arnie shrugged and mumbled something about trying a different spot, Ford decided that he wasn't going to make any more excuses but that he'd do what he wanted to do. After all, he was the skipper, and he didn't like having Arnie giving him the hairy eyeball every time he gave an order.

For Ford, the five-hour ride home was excruciatingly slow. He kept glancing at the clock on the bulkhead and moaning. To kill time, he put the boat on autopilot and helped Arnie dress the fish, gutting them and washing them down and then putting them in the fish box and shoveling ice on them. "Twenty-five hundred," said Ford, looking at the fish in the fish box. "Two thousand," said Arnie, scrubbing blood off the transom with a scrub brush. "Should be three."

Ford let the cover close with a bang and went back to the helm.

Then it was Arnie's watch so Ford went below and lay on his bunk and spent the entire time thinking of Sue, his heart beating so fast, he couldn't fall asleep. First he wanted to cry, and he even laughed out loud once when he imagined coming into port and seeing her on the dock and grabbing her and hugging her. By the time it was his watch, the sun was going down and the sea was apricot and purple and a planet gleamed on in the northeastern sky and he imagined it glowing over where she was on the shore at that moment. He ignored Mike, who sneaked up behind him and lapped his palm. By the time they reached Nantucket Sound, a moth-eaten gibbous moon, lying on its back, was sinking into the water on the horizon, grinning at him drunkenly, as if it were taunting him. It took forever for the moon to sink out of sight, but not as long as it seemed to take the diamond lights along the shore of the Cape to grow nearer. He was aching to be ashore.

When they reached the inner harbor, it was eight o'clock. Lights from buildings around the harbor like miniature moons made paths on the ripply water. As they passed the gas dock and glided past the end of the town dock where the fishing boats tied up, he searched for her, not seeing her at first, then spied her standing at the end of the pier, silhouetted by a light above a piling. Ford backed the boat into the slip and Arnie tossed the stern line to Sue. It fell short and she pranced to the edge of the dock to scoop it up. She was slim and dark-haired and wore red lipstick and white tennis shoes and a big T-shirt Ford had given her that said IN COD WE TRUST on the front and cutoff jean shorts that showed off her thighs to nice effect. Ford put the boat into neutral and raced out of the pilothouse, Mike in pursuit, and leapt onto the dock. He and Sue dovetailed into each other, he bending well over and she facing up to him, her slender arms not reaching all the way around his back, her dark hair dangling from the back of her head. They kissed and clung and mumbled and kissed and clung and mumbled and then began walking, joined together, toward the parking lot. Mike, his tail wagging his body, circled around them until Sue put out her hand and said, "Hi, Mike. Good boy, Mike." The dog rubbed up against her and beat his tail against their legs.

"It's just like I imagined," Ford said. "I was thinking about this offshore . . . how wonderful it would be to see you on the dock."

"Hey, Don," called Arnie, who was tying the spring line. "What about the fish?"

Ford looked back at him as though he had just remembered some long-forgotten dream.

"Ice them down again," he called back over his shoulder. "We'll unload in the morning."

"It's early. George'll still be there."

But Ford didn't answer. He bent back to Sue and they staggered as one toward his pickup, Mike trotting happily at their heels.

In the month of August, he had missed more days except for foul weather than he had since he had bought his boat twelve years before. Arnie had packed his grungy old seabag and said he had to sign on with another boat. "It's a matter of economics," he said. Ford understood. Arnie told him he couldn't make a living waiting to go offshore. "I'd still go with you when you feel like fishing again," he said. They shook hands. Arnie mussed Mike's head and gave him a quick scratch behind the ears. "Take care of Casanova," he said.

Ford tied up the *Sea Sprite* and locked the pilothouse door and spent his days and nights with Sue ashore. They went to the beach. Sometimes they went to restaurants for lunch or dinner. Other times, they stayed around Ford's house, where Sue now had all her belongings that she had brought with her from New York, and sat out in the sunny yard by the wild rosebushes that grew myriad tiny pink blossoms. They crept up the old stairs hand in hand to Ford's hot bedroom, where the open windows let in the scent of roses, hot grass, and ocean. Sue was a medical illustrator at a hospital in New York. She drew various parts of the anatomy, various instruments, various processes for various hospital publications. She had taken an extra two weeks of unpaid vacation to stay with Ford.

"It's funny that I got wrapped up with a fisherman," she said one still, warm afternoon as they sat in the old wood lawn chairs by the rosebushes. "I like to walk along the East River sometimes and look back across the river at Astoria, where I grew up. When I was a kid, I used to look at Manhattan from the other side. It was the city to us. I used to watch the tugs and barges and freighters even back then and wondered what men who made their living from the sea were like, where they came from. Now I know." Ford didn't say it, but he had the deep-water fisherman's well-earned snobbery and thought tugs that never went out of sight of land were a pretty poor comparison with those boats that ventured far offshore, out of sight of land for days at a time.

"My favorite place to walk is Carl Schurz Park," she told him. "It's not far from my apartment. You can look out and see the lighthouse on Roosevelt Island. At night, behind you, the city looks like a gigantic ocean liner—the way it looked when I lived on Crescent Street, only closer, more overwhelming."

He pressed her for details, drinking in her descriptions of the river, the views, and closed his eyes, imagining himself there with her. He loved her soft-spokenness and her directness, her sudden passionate descriptions of things she loved, the pungent comments that cracked like whips.

One time he had taken her out on *Sea Sprite* to fish for bass off Nantucket. They spent the day on a rip off Sankaty, close enough to shore to see the houses lining the bluff that looked like a gallery of Hopper paintings. On rod and reel, they caught ten big striped bass that he called pajama fish because of their stripes. Sue loved it, she said; she could see how he'd love doing this every day, and he said he couldn't do anything any day if it wasn't with her. Besides, this was bassing, he said, not codfishing, which was meat fishing, one step away from factory work.

"I could look at this forever," she said, staring at the cottages on the distant bluff. "Look at that light!"

The summer light was changing as the earth moved toward the autumn equinox, and Ford saw the changes in the color of the water and the sky and the slant of sunlight on their excursions four-wheeling on Nauset Beach. The day was approaching—the day they didn't want to bring up. But they had both been thinking about it and an invisible rope was tightening inside them.

One brilliant day that only the late summer or early fall offers like a gift before the cold, they drove to a remote end of Nauset Beach. There were only the beach, the bright, shiny green dune grass that described arcs in the sand like compasses, and the navy blue sea with its few dancing whitecaps. The pickup was parked beside them. Mike lay curled up in its shade. Lying low on their blanket on the beach, the sound of the surf sounded like periodic bursts of muffled applause.

"I love the way you look," she said, tickling the underside of his bicep with a tuft of dried seaweed. With his hands locked behind his head, he squinted at her in the sunshine. She was lying on her belly, her legs idly dangling upward in the air. She wore dark glasses. Her toenails were painted red. She wore a white Speedo one-piece bathing suit and her hair was caught back loosely with an elastic band.

He watched the two smooth, tan sides of her back and the muscles working beneath her skin. A few grains of sand speckled her back. The tiny hairs were bleached blond from sun and salt water.

And she said, "I love the way you *are*."

He looked from Sue's back across the hot sand to the water and the horizon. *Don't think about it,* he thought. *Don't think about having to go back offshore.*

"And I love the way you smell," she said, flicking the seaweed away.

"What, like an old codfish?"

"No," she said. She inched toward him and tipped her glasses up on her head. She brushed her nose against the skin of his shoulder and sniffed.

"No, it's like fresh bread."

"And you smell like a coconut," he said. He reached out an arm and wrapped it around her shoulders. She laid her cheek against his chest and sighed. They listened to the surf and the calls of the arctic terns flying by overhead as they scouted for fish. Two terns hovered above the surf line, waiting to dive.

"Those terns fly all the way down to Argentina in the winter," he said. Tern shadows knifed over their bodies and rippled away over the sand. "From Cape Cod to Cape Horn." And then he decided to say it—or rather, something inside him made him say it: the words that they had to face. He said it so quietly that at first he thought she hadn't heard.

"What are we going to do in the winter?"

The surf ploshed on the beach. The sun burned down. A breeze with a different, more northerly edge in it rattled the grass, causing each blade to throw off silver light. He was going to let it drop. Maybe he hadn't said it. Maybe he had only thought it.

But then she said, "I don't know . . . I don't know," so softly, it was almost drowned out by the surf. He stroked the nape of her neck, just under the soft weight of her hair, and saw the iridescence in each strand. "I'll probably be back in New York," she said, "and

you'll be offshore with your fish. Go where we need to go. Like the
terns." She lifted her head and pulled her glasses down and rolled
over on her back beside him on the blanket. "I don't want to talk
about it," she said, folding her arms.

He looked out to sea and thought of the trips offshore he had
taken when he had met her—only weeks before, although now it
seemed so long ago!—and how strangled he had felt, at the helm
with the hauling door wide open, as he looked across the miles of
dark water to the minute ruby lights of the radio towers on Nantucket about to drop off the horizon. To be without her for a minute, let alone nearly two straight days and nights, was torture. Every
moment without her was empty, and he had promised himself that
it would not happen again, that he could not stand being away from
her.

If it meant giving up fishing, his boat, his way of life, so be it.
Anything to be by her side. And at the thought of giving up everything for someone, he felt a surge of excitement instead of the despair that he assumed he would feel. He wanted to give himself to
someone, and the someone was this dark-haired, precise, gentle,
chestnut-eyed dove named Sue Callas.

"I'll move to New York," he said. He didn't move a muscle
after he heard himself say it. She didn't move. It was as if he hadn't
said it, so he said it again. "I could move to New York. I could find
a job there." He had no idea what kind of job he could find in New
York, and he felt faintly ridiculous having said it. What kind of jobs
were there for fishermen in Manhattan?

As if answering himself, he said, "It's an island, right? Maybe
I could . . ." He was going to say "get a job on a boat." And he
glanced at her and saw that she had taken off her dark glasses and
was looking at him. She blinked, closing her long lashes over her
eyes, and then looked at him again, her eyes moist.

"You'd hate it there," she said. "You'd hate it so much you'd
hate me."

He sat up on one elbow. "No, no I wouldn't. We'll make it work. It'll work out. Sue, we can't just go away from each other, say 'see ya' like we were kids. It'd be stupid. Look what we have." He took her in his arms and held her and then he felt her crying and he said, "Oh, jeeze, I didn't mean to." She sniffled and said, "*I* didn't mean to."

She sniffled for a while and then she looked up at him and smiled. It was the first time he had seen her cry. It was like a little girl's weeping. And the feeling that he was holding someone who quite possibly needed him made him say, "Sue, then why don't you move here with me? Sue"—and now he felt his heart and his tongue working in collusion without seeking counsel from his brain—he whispered, "Sue, I love you. I you you," he stuttered, then laughed and said, "I want you to . . . I want to marry you."

There was a moment when everything hung in suspension. No wave broke. No tern called. The breeze held its breath. The grasses stopped perfecting their arcs in the sand. The moment was suspended, stretched, alert to what Sue Callas was going to say.

For a long time, she had nothing to say. Then the impatient breeze could wait no longer and began working the grasses like styluses. The surf broke and the terns fluttered at the surf line and arrowed downward and rose, flapping, silvery fish wriggling between their beaks.

And then she whispered, "Oh, Donny." And that was all. She got up, not looking at him, looking out to sea. She said apologetically, "I'm a little cold." He got up and went over to the pickup and pulled his sweatshirt out from the front seat. He went back over to her, feeling as if he were floating. She had an odd sad smile on her face as she put the sweatshirt on. She rested a cool hand on his arm and said, "Donny, I'm sorry. Do you mind if I go for a walk . . . by myself?"

She went down to the surf line and let the foam run up and wash her ankles as she walked. Mike burst from underneath the truck and galloped down to her, bounded at her, and then settled down to trot beside her when he saw that she was not in a playful mood. Ford watched her in the oversized gray sweatshirt, with her fine legs and tousled hair, and saw that she was looking hard at the sea, glancing down only every now and then as a wave ran up to her and splashed her legs. Mike let the waves chase him. The sun was getting lower.

Ford stood paralyzed on the blanket as he watched her recede, thinking only, *What have I done? I've ruined everything.* He thought of what he was going to give her tonight—the package he had so carefully wrapped and hidden behind the seat, the package that now seemed destined to stay there.

She disappeared around a curve in the beach. Ford took his surf pole from the back of the pickup and tied on a jig and began casting methodically for something to take his mind off what he had done. But his mind was already numb. He flogged the water and felt as though the world consisted only of him and Sue and that suddenly everything had changed. He lied to himself that he hadn't thought about asking her to marry him before, that he had blurted it only because of the beauty of the day and the beauty of their love and his fear of losing her to the season. But he caught himself in the lie. He had, in fact, imagined asking her to marry him, the way he had imagined meeting her on the dock. He hadn't felt this way about any of the other women he had known. There was really no explanation. He simply felt something different being around her.

What was different was that this new feeling gave him a kind of emotional influenza. Without Sue, how would he recover? Would the feeling fade when she was gone, simply run its course, leave him with a memory of what it was like to be feverishly in love—viewed through the cool, sober eyes of someone no longer in love? What would happen now? Now that the fever had made him so delirious, had he ruined everything by taking his fantasies seriously? Her reaction gave him a kind of seasickness he had never felt at sea. Would she simply walk away?

The sun sat orange on the dunes before she returned. They said nothing, but held each other, and the hug restored Ford's hope. The sand underfoot was cooling and felt like velvet, and her small body wrapped in his arms made him feel a loss along with the hope.

"Let's go," she said. He looked into her eyes, imploring her to say something, but his fear had grown so that he didn't want to ask her what she was thinking for fear that it was the thing that he feared. He shook off the blanket as she got in the pickup. Mike jumped into the back. Ford scanned the horizon, a habit of his, and saw there a white-hulled vessel. He wondered who it was and what they were after and how much fish they had aboard.

They had dinner that night at the place where they had met only a month before, Skipper's, a tiny rustic place on a harbor. Mike waited outside in the pickup.

They sat at a table with a plastic red-and-white-checkered tablecloth by the open window that overlooked the harbor.

"Remember?" said Ford, giving her a quick glance. "It seems so long ago."

"But it wasn't, Donny," she said. She shook her head, closed her eyes, and then looked out the window. "That's the problem. It wasn't long ago. You've fantasized everything about us," she said, then gave an exasperated laugh. "I feel like I can't talk to you about all this. It's all so much more complicated than it has to be."

She looked at him. "I'm confused about everything. You've confused me. I don't want to have to face this. I feel terrible about how I'm making you feel, terrible about how I feel."

She fell silent and Ford looked out at the boats in the harbor.

"Oh, Donny," she said, taking his hand. "You must be thinking I'm deliberately making your life miserable. I won't even tell you how I feel about you asking me to marry you."

Ford looked at her and thought how different this time was from the first time they had been in Skipper's.

And she said, "If you knew me better, you'd know why I won't tell you how I feel."

"Then tell me," he said. "Tell me why you won't tell me."

"Because I'm too confused to tell you how I feel."

In late July, he had stopped at Skipper's for a chocolate frappe on his way to get a load of ice before heading back offshore. Sue had come for a lobster roll. They were the only ones in the place besides Betty, the waitress, whom Ford had known since high school. It had been a hot morning, and it was still only eleven o'clock. But the inside of Skipper's was breezy, the windows open to the harbor. The place had only a few tables and a soda counter with stools, but covering the walls was a mass of sea paraphernalia, from huge lobster claws with the dates of their demise written on them with Magic Marker, to pictures of Skipper's buried in snow, to mounted trophy striped bass, their mouths agape, to net and line and lobster traps and buoys. It was like eating in a fisherman's shanty. The difference between Skipper's and a tourist trap was that the junk here was real and had once been used.

On a shelf above the counter where Sue was eating her lobster roll were three round objects as big as dinner plates. They were mosaics made out of shells—periwinkles and moonsnails and scallop shells and quahog shells. The shells were glued to the round wooden plates to form different scenes. One was a schooner; one was a modern fishing boat; one was the shape of Cape Cod.

When Ford had come in, Sue was asking Betty about the mosaics. Ford stepped inside and stood beside her. They smiled at each other, and for a moment it seemed as if Sue had stopped listening to Betty talking about what she called sailor's valentines.

Betty said hi to Ford and told Sue that in whaling days sailors used to make these mosaics from the shells they found on the exotic islands they visited on long voyages and brought them back for their wives or sweethearts. It was a craft to pass the time, like scrimshaw.

"My grandmother still makes these," she said. "She does a beautiful job, old as she is. My kids bring her the shells. It's about the only useful thing they do," she added, but she was smiling.

"I like the one of the fishing boat," said Sue. And then she asked Ford which one he liked the best.

"The chocolate frappe," he said.

Then there was talk about how hot it was outside and Sue said she was dog-tired from pedaling her bike all over the place all morning—and before you knew it, Ford offered to give her a ride, but only if she didn't mind stopping off for a load of ice first.

A seed had been planted in Ford's mind. And when he got back ashore after his next trip and he and Sue went out on their first date (their second, as he said, if you counted the trip to get the ice), the seed flowered: He paid a visit to Betty's grandmother and handed the old lady a snapshot of the *Sea Sprite*.

"A lovely boat," she said. "This for someone special?"

Ford smiled.

Donny," she said, "the problem is, we don't even know each other." Her fisherman's platter sat congealing in front of her. "You didn't have any idea how I'd react. How long have you been thinking about asking me?"

"Haven't you thought about it?"

She smiled. "Who wouldn't?"

"That's what I mean. You thought about it. I've been thinking about it. I just happened to be the one who did the asking."

"And I happen to be the one who's being confused."

When they had had enough of sitting, they left the dinners they had picked at and walked outside along the harbor, looking at the fishing boats in their slips. Mike trotted behind them. They went to the end of the jetty and gazed out over the water. Ford asked her if she didn't feel chilly and she said yes. He gave her his jacket and put his arm around her.

They walked down to the beach. Small waves rushed the beach and the smell of seaweed was thick. Clouds had moved in and the night was starless. The wind had shifted: southeast, a foul quadrant. They felt as though they were floating as they walked, their legs being almost invisible to them. There was also the smell of rain in the night air: a sudden change from the glorious weather during the day.

"I haven't been able to give you an answer," she said suddenly, as though they had never ceased talking. "I don't know what to do. You've got to understand. You really shook me. Do you always take everyone by surprise?"

All of the roiling emotion that Ford had been containing throughout the day threatened to burst forth. Did this mean that there was hope, after all? But now he found he could say nothing.

She said softly, "Donny, I love you, too. I've never felt this way before . . . about anyone."

With the first few words, his heart soared, but there was something in the tone of the last few words that made it dive. The tone said that she had made a decision.

"But all this—marriage, everything—Donny, I don't know how to put this. We've known each other for only a few weeks. You've flattered me and I love you for it, but it's not the right time. But I don't want you to think I don't love you, because I do."

Ford felt the rope inside him constricting. He opened his mouth to say something to her, to say the miraculous words that would change everything, that would bring back the spell.

"You know I've got to go back to the city," she said. "I don't want to, but I've got to. I can come back up on weekends. We'll see how things go."

What can I say to change her mind? He could sense that she was putting on a brave face about resuming her life, but what were the words that would help her remove the mask and see the truth of what she wanted? He envisioned her going back to New York, getting used to her life there again, letting the magic of their time together fade.

"It's big leap, Donny," she said, her voice fading. She rested her head against his shoulder. "It's just too big. My mom's still in Queens, alone. My job is in the city." She shivered. "I'm getting cold."

Cold feet, thought Ford. He moved as if in a trance, a dream of frustration in which he could think of all the words that would instantly change her mind and yet couldn't utter them. But he sensed also that anything he would say might make her shy away like some delicate woods animal.

"I don't mean to hurt you, Donny," she said. "I'm sorry. But we've got to give it some time."

There is no time, he thought. *There is no time, when I love you the way I do.*

But he couldn't say it.

"Don't leave" was all he could bring himself to say. "Part of me will be gone when you leave." And it made her cry.

He was letting her slip out of his grasp, he felt, as he watched her pack her belongings that night. They avoided the subject. He tried to make a joke, saying, "Don't forget to leave enough room for me in that suitcase," but it came out sounding forlorn.

That night, he lay awake beside her and then rose sometime in the middle of the night. Rain swept down and he listened to its syncopations as it ran in the gutters, tapped on the leaves, dripped from the eaves. He smelled the rain coming in the window.

He was watching her leave forever, he thought the next morning as he drove her to Hyannis and the bus that would take her to Providence and the train to New York. He had offered to drive her home, but she said she needed time to think.

"Mike," she said, patting the dog on the head, "take care of Donny."

He couldn't believe it was happening, but it was. He put her bag in the luggage bay. She looked as though she hadn't slept, either, and her mouth was set in a thin line. They held each other and then she said, "I'll call you when I get in." Then she was on the bus. He saw her in the window. She was crying and she waved him away. Leave now, she seemed to be saying, don't look at me like this.

The rest of the day, he found himself in different places, feeling as though he had just awakened to find her gone. The seat in his pickup was empty except for Mike. The house was empty. She wasn't sketching in one of the chairs out by the rosebush. She wasn't anywhere, yet she was everywhere. He remembered a homily he had heard long ago. The priest had said the dead are kept alive by our memory of them. They live. He stood looking out the window at the two empty chairs and the dead buds on the rosebush nodding in the gray light and he heard someone moaning: himself. And he thought, *Memory is killing me.*

Mike came up behind him and pressed a wet nose against his palm.

He couldn't stand staying in the house by himself, so he went down to the harbor to check on the boat. The other boats were in because the weather offshore was foul. He went onto *Sea Sprite* and stood in the pilothouse remembering their day bassing off Nantucket. He remembered all the days: picnics on the beach, her way of peeling an orange so that the rind was in one piece, like a spring. He remembered the way her skin felt, the coconut smell of her skin with the suntan lotion on it. The gloss of her hair and her way of tracing the lines of his face with her forefinger. The chestnut color of her eyes. The heat of her kisses. Her saying that she could spend the rest of her life in this place, with the beauty of the Cape all around her. Her wish that she could paint some of the places they had visited together.

Someone thudded aboard.

"Hey, Don, how's it going?" It was Arnie. Mike wagged his way over to him. Arnie's orange oilskins were dripping and his pointy beard was soaked. "You going out?"

Ford said he was going to listen to the weather and make up his mind.

"We're getting ready to go," said Arnie. "They're saying rain, but this wind's supposed to drop. Where's Sue?"

He couldn't look at Arnie. He turned to the radar, pretending to check it, and said, "Oh, she's in New York. Had to go back for a while."

Arnie was still looking at him as he fiddled with knobs. Ford turned and looked at him.

"What are you looking at?"

"Nothing. Didn't let that one get away, did you?"

"What do you mean by that?"

"You two seemed made for each other. Christ, you were like Siamese twins."

Ford came to the verge of letting the rope unravel, of spilling his guts, of pouring out every constrained bit of emotion to Arnie, to tell him how godforsaken desperate he felt, how destitute, how dead without her.

But all he said was, "Well, you know. Things change." And yet he didn't believe it.

He went back home and wouldn't look at the telephone, having decided that it wouldn't ring, that it would never ring again. He listened to the weather on the radio three times. He looked out all the windows, Mike following behind. But at four o'clock, it rang. It was Sue and she said, "I can't believe how much I miss you. It was the longest train ride in history."

"The longest day in history."

"I don't know why I left."

"Neither do I."

"I just felt that I had to."

"That's okay."

"I wasn't going to call. But I couldn't stand not hearing you."

"I think I would have gone crazy if you hadn't called."

There was a silence and then Ford said, "What are we going to do?"

She said, "I still don't know, Donny. Give it some time. We've got to give it some time."

When they eventually hung up, he felt elated for a few hours and then suddenly plunged into his newfound despair. But he knew he couldn't keep dragging himself around the house, waiting for something to happen that wasn't going to happen. The weather wasn't going to be great, but it wasn't dirty—or *doity,* as Sue would have pronounced it.

The next morning by seven, he had the boat fueled up, iced up, and supplied with groceries. He hadn't taken a trip offshore by himself for years, though he used to do it regularly when he first started out. He was planning to go out and fish till dark and then anchor up on the Fishing Rip, sleep overnight, fish the next day, and come back in by early afternoon. He filled up the auxiliary fuel tank in case he wanted to stay out longer. Maybe in a few weeks he could convince Arnie to come back to work for him. He finished unloading supplies and drove the pickup from the pier up to the lot and parked it with other fishermen's trucks.

He was pulling his seabag out from the back of the seat when he spotted the package from Betty's grandmother. He had never given it to Sue. The sight of it made his heart pound and dive. It was the sailor's valentine that Betty's grandmother had made for him, constructed from shells collected on the beaches. It was a portrait of his own boat, and made out in shells beneath the boat that was bounding through the water was "Sea Sprite."

As he went toward his boat, carrying the valentine, he thought that if he had given it to her, somehow it would have made things different. Now it was a useless object, and he put it on the bulkhead above the helm as a kind of shrine to his own lack of courage.

As he passed the outer jetty and headed into Nantucket Sound, doubts crowded around him: He wondered whether giving her the sailor's valentine would have made any difference. Once, she had said that tokens like rings and boxes of candy weren't her style.

"I feel like a squaw when someone buys me that stuff," she said. "Doing trade in trinkets."

He passed Monomoy Point and headed into the Atlantic swells. He set a course south by southeast for the Great South Channel and the codfish grounds, staring past the windshield wiper at the rainy gray sea. Maybe if he had given her the sailor's valentine, it would have made things even worse.

But how would he ever know if he didn't get to know her better? He decided that she was right, after all: They didn't know each other all that well. He didn't even know what her reaction would be to a present!

But they weren't ever going to get to know each other being apart.

It took another hour of steaming through the lumpy swells and rain for an idea to reveal itself to Ford.

At first, he dismissed it. But then it took up residence in his mind and he began picturing how it would work. It wasn't impossible. If the weather held, it would be easy. The only thing he would have to fight was boredom.

Suddenly he felt lighter on his feet, lighter of heart, his soul filled with light. Was it a crazy idea? It probably was. But the fact that he was going to do something, take some action, made things seem possible again.

He reset the autopilot due south and ran below to dig through the locker with the old charts. He found what he was looking for: a mildewed chart covering Block Island Sound south along the Atlantic side of Long Island and the approaches to New York that he had bought a few years back when he and Arnie were thinking about going after tilefish in the depths off Long Island. At ten knots, his top cruising speed, he figured it would take him around thirty hours, and after thirty hours, he would have his arms around her again.

"Put on your street shoes," he said to Mike. "We're going to New York."

Off Montauk doubts began deviling him. Where would he tie up the *Sea Sprite* when he arrived? He knew the shipping traffic would be heavy in the approaches and the rivers of New York. He calculated that he would arrive in the daytime, even after he laid up off Southampton to catch a few hours of sleep, which was good, because he knew how incredibly difficult it was to navigate when you were faced with an unfamiliar night horizon filled with lights. He was staying out of the shipping lanes and had had no trouble with shipping traffic. So far the weather had held. Rain fell periodically, but the visibility was over three miles. The wind was light, the seas choppy.

Still, it was the season of hurricanes and gales. Would he make the run beyond Long Island without taking the pasting of his life?

And when he arrived, what then? He struggled to stay awake and watched the gray water blend into the gray horizon as the *Sea Sprite* forged on.

Doubts gnawed deeper the second night as he fought to stay awake. Was this the world's most insane idea? To steam for days without even letting her know he was coming? Was it too late to turn back?

At about eleven o'clock, he decided to put a call through and raised the New York marine operator on the radio. He got through—to her answering machine. He didn't mention that he was miles and miles at sea when he left his message.

He steamed on. Every few hours, Mike emerged from the cabin and looked at him soulfully and then turned around and went below again. The night seemed endless.

Around two o'clock, he got the marine operator again and put through a call. This time, as the answering machine was taking his message, a gravel-voiced Sue picked up.

"Donny," she said.

Ford was flying. He tried to keep himself in check. He knew he was delirious from lack of sleep. He had to watch what he would say. His heart was hammering in his chest.

"Sue, honey," he said, his voice crossing over the night ocean and through the ozone from the tiny boat to her bedside table. "Sue, I'm on my way."

"You're on your way," she said. He knew that she smelled of that rich, warm human smell of sleep and that her entire body was heavy and supple with it. "You're on your way where?" she mumbled.

"I'll be in New York tomorrow," he said. "I wanted it to be a surprise. But I couldn't wait to tell you."

His heart hammered so hard, it hurt as the silence grew. Was she excited? Why wasn't she saying anything?

"Sue . . ."

"Donny," she said, nearly whispering. "It's so soon."

The hammering turned to grinding. There was a long silence.

"Sue, I can't . . . I've got to see you."

There was a short silence. "Where are you? You sound like . . . Are you calling from your boat?"

He said he was. He could hear some sounds over the radio that told him she was sitting up.

"You took your boat all the way from the Cape?"

He looked out through the wet windshield at the blackness of the night before him.

"Not quite all the way. With luck, I'll be in New York tomorrow."

"I can't believe it, Donny. It's so far."

What she said next made his heart leap again.

"You're crazy," she said with a laugh. "You're absolutely crazy."

He told her that he would call her again when he got to a wharf or a marina sometime during the late morning, if all went well.

"Donny?" she said before she hung up.

"Uh-huh?" he said.

And she said softly, "I can't wait to see you." And then she laughed again and said, "I can't believe it. You're crazy!"

The next few hours, he was buoyed by her words and wider awake than he had been for a day. But it wasn't much longer before fatigue and doubt began to overcome him and make him wonder if in fact he wasn't crazy, not just crazy in love. Maybe Sue would think he was making a grandstand play, that he'd have a wild few hours with her and something to tell the boys back home and then he'd turn around and steam back to the Cape and the surprises would all be over.

"Crazy," he said to Mike. "Maybe I'm just plain crazy."

But he was so exhausted by the time he reached Rockaway Point that he had to forgo even the effort to doubt himself in order to stay awake and on course.

He had never felt so puny as when he finally passed beneath the Verrazano-Narrows Bridge. He admired the little *Sea Sprite* more than ever for having brought him so far without a protest or a problem. Out of the thick mist that had replaced the rain, the bridge loomed so huge, it looked like some monstrous specter, a dream out of science fiction, like a city suspended in the air that spanned planets.

Container ships and tugs and garbage scows swept by out of the mist. The chatter on the radio sounded continuous. The water itself was filled with whirlpools left by the huge ships' propeller wash and their wakes and gave off a thick cold stew stench of humanity and brine.

Then the island of Manhattan appeared, looking, from his vantage point on the water, like the base ramparts of a city built above the clouds, since the skyscrapers disappeared halfway up into the mist. It seemed like a great bizarre ship steaming toward him. The Statue of Liberty was a pale green ghost, insignificant compared with the mass of buildings rising out of the water.

He was forced to change course to avoid the Staten Island ferry, a vessel that resembled a fat floating harmonica. He made his way up the East River. He passed wharf after wharf on the Brooklyn side and steered beneath the Brooklyn Bridge, the Manhattan Bridge, the Williamsburg Bridge, and the Queensboro Bridge, the forty-foot *Sea Sprite* feeling small as a cork. The tide was fair and his speed was twelve knots. To port, the city raced by the *Sea Sprite* as though it were an ocean liner passing a gull. And he remembered what Sue had said about the city, how it seemed to her that it was like an ocean liner, too.

He took the port channel beneath the Queensboro Bridge, keeping Roosevelt Island to his right. Weary from the long passage but coursing now with nervous energy, Ford ran his burning eyes along the shoreline of Manhattan and almost missed it, a landmark that Sue had told him about, to his other side: At the tip of Roosevelt Island stood the lighthouse she had described to him—the one opposite the park where she liked to walk.

He throttled down and looked up at the cityscape. He was beside a sort of promenade. He steered the *Sea Sprite* closer. The shore was rocks and atop that was a railing. There were trees behind that and then buildings. Even though it was one o'clock, only a few people huddled under umbrellas strolled in the mist along the promenade.

He idled along farther, trying to decide where he would put in. He knew from what she had told him that she lived and worked not far from here. But he couldn't put in and leave *Sea Sprite* on this shore. He decided he would go through Hell Gate to one of the marinas in Queens and was about to set a new course when he drew parallel to the northernmost point of the promenade and saw a lone figure standing there. The figure stood still, as if on lookout at the bow of a ship. Suddenly Mike scrambled out of the pilothouse and galloped up forward to the bow and began barking.

"Mike, get back here!" yelled Ford, opening the hauling door and sticking his head out. But Mike kept on barking, and the person standing on the promenade moved to face the sound of the dog barking. Ford brought the boat closer, and Mike kept barking, wagging himself in two and shooting looks back at Ford.

The person's umbrella slipped to one side and then dropped to the ground, and it was then that Ford saw who it was. He ran forward, calling "Sue!Sue!Sue!" and laughing and waving his arms and feeling light as a star. Sue was laughing and holding her hands

to her mouth and then she was climbing over the railing. Ford ran
below and grabbed a length of line, then ran back topside to cleat it
to the anchor post.

"Donny!" she shouted. Her hair was soaked. She shucked off
her heels and picked her way down the wet rocks in her stockings.
Ford heaved the line to her and she pranced for it and caught it and
made it fast to the railing post. He jumped back to the helm. She
inched down to the edge of the water, staying above the level of the
boat.

Ford maneuvered the boat as close as he dared to the rocks
and ran out on deck to wait for a swell to bring the *Sea Sprite's* stern
to its highest point.

"Hang on," he called to her. "Wait for a wave." He looked
back down the river for a swell.

The stern began to lift. The swell was cresting and he turned
back toward her. As he reached his arms out to catch her, he saw
that she had not moved. She was watching him. In her look, he saw
that something was holding her back, holding her to her rock, her
place, her island.

"Now!" he called. "Jump now!"

The stern stood high and steady. *She must jump now,* he
thought. *She must jump now.*

And he watched her pale face, wet with rain, suspended
against the sky.

THE SHEARWATER

The old man, no longer in need of an alarm clock, woke in the dark with a dream of snow still fresh in his mind. He reached for his glasses on the bedside table, put them on, and lay under the covers, listening to his wife's breathing. The air in the room was cold on the tip of his nose, the bed sleep-warm, the cat at the end of the bed a curled warm weight.

Forty-seven years with his wife and he was still unable to tell whether she was awake or not. Sometimes Martha was snoring and seconds later she was asking him if he felt all right or was telling him to be careful or was reminding him to call her when he got to Monomoy Point. This morning, she lay on her side, facing him, her breathing smooth and regular and gentle, as natural in her sleep as an animal.

A mystery, thought Warren. *Awake or asleep, a mystery I'll never solve.*

"Martha?" he whispered. Her breathing went on as before. He let her sleep, staying in bed only long enough to say two Our Fathers and two Hail Marys, the way he began every day before going to sea or working ashore.

Then he eased his body out of the bed, the old wood floorboards shrunken with the night's cold cracking under his weight.

He took care to replace the blankets over his spot to keep the warmth around his wife. He slept in a pair of ancient red flannel pajamas that had been washed so much that they were now the pale pink of sun-bleached lobster shells. He moved through the dark room, penguinlike in his stiffness, his heavy muscles still asleep, his joints complaining.

He went into the bathroom, where he had hung his work clothes from a hook on the back of the door the night before. The routine was an ancient one, unconscious, performed like a rite over decades. He took his time shaving, careful not to nick himself. Then he unbuttoned his pajamas, his hard, thick fingers so callused that he could barely feel the buttons, and then bent to the work of putting on enough clothes to keep him warm through a winter's day fishing. Long johns, two pairs of wool socks, khaki work pants, a flannel shirt and a plaid wool shirt, and his old khaki work cap, worn in all but the most extreme cold, went on in slow but meticulous succession. Then he shut off the light and felt his way to the head of the stairs, where his eyes caught light coming from downstairs and his ears picked up the crackle of a radio: Martha had risen while he dressed and had gone silently downstairs to start the coffee and listen to the weather. He thumped down the stairs one at a time, his joints not yet limber but his body warming in its cocoon of clothes.

They didn't talk at first. Her long gray hair that had once been jet black was piled up loosely and carelessly on her head like a sweep of tall windswept grasses. Her gray eyes met his when he came into the bright room—and that was their greeting, a look of warmth that passed between them.

On the radio, a voice was saying, "All stations reporting snow." The report went on to describe conditions up and down the New England coast and surrounding seas. The wall clock read 12:45 A.M.

Warren sat down at the kitchen table and said, "I dreamed about snow last night."

Martha poured a cup of coffee for her husband and set it in front of him. She sat down and smoothed a place mat with the flat of her hand.

"Where're you headed today?" she said, and added quickly, "Not after that gear."

Warren took a sip of coffee.

"No, I thought I'd head to Orion, where Lester hit them yesterday. Start there, anyway."

"Don't you go sneaking offshore to get that gear, either."

"No, wouldn't think of it."

"Yes you would." She was smiling at him.

"I know I would, but I won't."

A northeaster two weeks before had hit and Warren had been unable to check his lobster traps since. They were set over a hundred miles offshore on the continental shelf, where he, his son, Gary, and another crewman spent most of the spring, summer, and fall lobstering. But it was too dangerous to go so far in so small a boat all winter, so Warren pursued other fish, codfish mostly, and in the spring halibut. He wouldn't go haul the gear any way you looked at it: Gary had left for Colorado and his winter job plowing snow for the ski areas, the crewman was sick, and every time Warren found a decent replacement crewman, the weather had turned too dirty to make the trip.

"Well, thanks for the coffee, Martha dear."

They both stood up, Warren pecking her on the cheek, she taking his coffee cup to the sink. He headed to the mudroom to put on his coat, and then checked the pockets for his tobacco pouch and pipe. Martha was looking out the black kitchen window. Enough light spread out to illuminate the fine snowflakes that twirled down outside.

"Look, Warren, isn't it pretty?"

He turned. Martha lifted herself up slightly on her toes to see
out, and he saw his wife, the woman now aged and gray, wrapped
in her old terry-cloth robe, and he saw also the lively dark-haired
girl he had married half a century before.

He smiled.

"Yes, it is," he said, putting a hand on the doorknob. "It's
very pretty."

Carrying the small cooler containing his breakfast, lunch, dinner, and a thermos of coffee, Warren stepped out of the mudroom
onto the porch. Underfoot lay two inches of dry, fluffy snow. The
snow whispered down. He sniffed the iron cold air and listened for
a breeze in the tops of the pines beyond the locust grove and the
barn, but there was no sound save that of the snow against his coat.
He took the steps carefully, the dusty snow creaking and cracking
under his work boots. He walked out of the circle of light cast by
the outside light and went to his pickup truck. Snow powdered
away from the window as he opened the door. He started the engine and let it warm up as he brushed the snow off the truck as
easily as if he was puffing away feathers. When he pulled onto the
unplowed road, the outside light flicked on and off twice.

The ride to the harbor at this time of day was one of his
favorite parts of being a fisherman. It made him different from and
much luckier than most other people. He went places and saw
creatures day after day that most people never experienced first-
hand in all their lives. The whales and sharks and porpoises and
skies and stars and seas and storms were one thing. Even when he
was ashore, just driving to his boat as he was now, he saw along the
roadsides the raccoons and possums and foxes and now the coyotes
that people abed only read about. He passed through the deserted
town of Harwich Port, at this hour left populated only by snowflakes and ghosts. He liked the off-season trip to the harbor the
most because it was the emptiest. During the summer, a few stray
drunken tourists would always break the peace of the deserted

hours. Sometimes he even let the truck ease into the left-hand lane for a mile or two and steered with nothing more than his right thumb.

When he got to the harbor, he felt a glad quickening of his pulse: Don's, Chet's, and Lester's boats were still in their slips. He loved being the first boat out, the first to hit the fish, the first to return with a load, the first to find a new market for a fish no one else was catching or even thought to catch. That he would be the first out of the harbor gave Warren a tremble of satisfaction. It was good to show the other fishermen that he was, as always, a step ahead of them.

Warren parked his truck. His was the only vehicle in the parking lot. He was doing something secret, vaguely illicit, like eloping. Leaving for the oceanic distances in the silent times of the night made him feel as if he was stealing away, that he should keep his voice low, make as little disturbance as possible.

He walked down through the parking lot, the snow a smooth expanse of white under the lone streetlight. He passed the fishermen's shanties that ran in a tumbledown row to the pier. The shanties were covered with snow, even their front shingles like ermine ruffles. Ahead were the boats in their slips. The snow lay like thick toothpaste on the spring lines and stern lines and bow lines. The tops of the pilings wore snowcaps except for the creneleated ones where gulls had landed. His boots made the snow creak and squeak. The small sounds made the darkness that surrounded the few lights—the one up at the parking lot and the two at either end of the pier—seem a limitless presence that Warren sensed beyond the lights, the boats, the falling snow. If Warren felt a connection from the world to the world beyond the world, he also felt an uneasiness with it, a hope for what lay beyond, and a kind of fear of the vastness—a grander one than what he felt for the fathoms that lay below the thin hull of his boat when he fished far offshore, a deeper, quieter fear that gave him vertigo.

He stepped aboard the snowy fantail of the *Nancy K.*, the boat that had taken him out and brought him back for the thirty seasons since his daughter was born. He stopped for a long moment to let the silence fill his soul. Here was one of the few places on the planet where silence remained. Even offshore, the silence was vanishing. The fleets of the big draggers broke up the schools and killed the fishing. Along the high-tide lines on the beaches, spent tampon applicators and hypodermics outnumbered the driftwood and seashells.

He let the snowflakes whisk his face. He listened to the snowflakes whisper against his hat and coat. The way the snow played at his face, touching and tickling almost as if it were curious, took him back to when his daughter was little. Holding her in his lap, he would let her steal his glasses. She would pull at his ears, laughing her freewheeling laugh, talking her own language. But then she would grow serious and examine his face carefully, using her tiny fingertips to feel what she saw. Now she was a grown woman with a husband and two children of her own.

Warren unlocked the padlock on the pilothouse door and thought, *Time to break the silence.* For the next twelve hours, the sound of a sixteen-cylinder diesel engine would dominate his ears. No other sound save that of the radio could overcome that of the great deafening metallic beast, the beast of burden that was also the deliverer—if the diesel roared you made it home. Silence offshore was the loud reminder of the proximity of death.

The diesel came to life with a giant's clearing of the throat and loudly muttered into an idle. Faint shivers surrounded the hull of the *Nancy K.* Chunks of snow fell off the lines like sailors abandoning a ship.

Warren went through his routine: He listened to the weather again (light and variable winds, no change), checked the oil (full), checked the fuel (full), checked the batteries (okay), turned on the radar, the loran, made sure the fish finder had a fresh roll of paper, checked the compass, the automatic pilot, and finally his hand lines, the only gear he figured he would use on this day's trip. Then he stepped aft and lighted his pipe. He puffed and watched the smoke drift up as the snow fell down. If the wind stayed down, he thought he might just go offshore to look for the gear, not haul it, mind you—no one said anything about hauling it—but just to find it. The way he figured it, he had about three thousand dollars somewhere out in a canyon on the continental shelf, and he could use it.

The snow feathered off the lines as he uncleated them and cast off. He guided the boat around the pilings and out past the boatworks buildings and glanced one last time at the parking lot. No one else had arrived. He would be out fifteen, probably thirty minutes ahead of the rest of them. *If the lazy slobs go out at all,* he thought, chuckling to himself.

He passed the channel buoy and throttled up. Ahead was nothing but blackness and snow pinwheeling into the windshield. He navigated by radar and loran only and would do so all day if the snow fell as densely as it fell now. With the seas so calm, the ride was serene and routine. The only thing to fight was boredom. His many years of going to sea had purged him of the need for sleep. He knew this was unusual. He was wary of crewmen on their watches, especially newcomers. During the night watches, he many times came topside from his bunk to sit with the crewman and talk to him, to keep him company and to gauge his true abilities.

His course took him from the harbor across Nantucket Sound to Monomoy Point, and from Monomoy to the open ocean. To Warren the open ocean wasn't an expanse of watery vastness, but a familiar area with places he knew by the character and contour of their bottom, as if he was looking at a hill or a steambed or an outcrop of rock. Over here there was the Mussels, there the Channel, over there the Crushed Shells, out there the Northern Edge, not to mention the rips like Tomahawk and Half Moon, Asia Rip and Old Man Shoal, Handkerchief Shoal and Bearse's, Orion and the Rose and Crown and Pollock Rip. Each one was different at different times of the day, tide, moon, and year. Weather changed them. In a swollen notebook on the console above the helm, Warren jotted down their coordinates and where he caught fish on them and how they looked to him. The familiar places encompassed an area that stretched from Massachusetts Bay to Nova Scotia, Georges Bank to the backside of Nantucket, Truro to the continental shelf.

He radioed Martha at the Point, as he always did, to tell her he had decided to head to the Fishing Rip, since it was so flat, the weather report was good, and since the draggers had probably already slayed the fish that Lester had found yesterday. Draggers would move in on a spot even on a rip nowadays, the snags be damned. The bigger boats fished longer hours and took more risks to catch a diminishing amount of fish; the smaller boats fished in worse weather even in winter just to keep food in their families' mouths.

Rounding the Point, Warren listened in on two draggermen talking to each other on the radio, the usual garbled and profane complaints about dogfish and fouled nets. He nursed a hatred for the boats that dragged nets along the bottom, having lost so much gear to them over the years. The orange glow of the radar in his glasses, he watched the rabbit's paw mass of Monomoy disappearing behind him and picked up two blips just beyond the Great Round Shoal buoys—probably the draggers he had listened to over the radio.

He drank a cup of coffee, ate a ham sandwich, filled his cup again, and relighted his pipe beyond the double buoys at Great Round Shoal. The trip was so uneventful that he began calculating how long it would take him to reach the area where he had last seen his gear, how long it would take him to haul it if he found it, and how angry Martha would be if he went. He could haul one string himself, he decided; any more and he wouldn't be able to stack the traps properly on the afterdeck. He could be there at the latest ten o'clock with this following tide; spend four or five hours, if he needed it, hunting the buoys that marked the traps; haul a string and be home by ten or eleven. A good day's work if it meant salvaging gear, every bit as good as trying to jig for codfish that weren't there. He had plenty of fuel. It would be like the old days, he thought, the days when he depended only on himself. He would call Martha when he got down there.

So Warren set a new course for a farther place, a place a hundred miles offshore, a place measured in the hundreds of fathoms. He checked the radar and the loran, gave the engine more throttle, and relighted his pipe.

By daybreak the draggermen's radio chatter had dwindled and the snow had increased. In the dim light, Warren could now make out the forward section of the *Nancy K.* After so many hours of steaming in darkness with the orange radar, the cherry red numbers of the loran, and the compass light in his eyes, it was good to see solid objects. He felt he had emerged from an extended dream.

But visibility was decreasing even as the day grew lighter. A circle of green sea around the boat was all that Warren could see with the naked eye. As he steamed through the snow, he saw birds taking off at his approach. There were herring gulls and fulmars and even a gannet or two, but mostly there were shearwaters. Shearwaters were long-winged oceanic birds, like smaller albatrosses. They skimmed the troughs and crests of swells with their slender knife-like wings spread wide. They were astounding aerobats, gliding and maneuvering with grace and speed, but paddling on the water after fish guts tossed off a boat, they were irritable and aggressive. They fought over the guts, beeping and peering just underwater like scientists into telescopes, and they had tugs-of-war with intestines.

The *Nancy K.* bounded along, shooing shearwaters off their roosts on the water. It took Warren a minute to realize that on the radar screen, approaching from the northeast at a range of five

miles, the blip he had been watching was closing in on him. It was
big enough to be a coastal freighter, though if it was, it was danger-
ously off course: It was steaming straight through Nantucket
Shoals, the sandbar-fouled waters that lay between Nantucket and
the shipping lanes.

He double-checked the loran and scrutinized his chart: He
was bearing south southeast, east of the Fishing Rip—right where
he was supposed to be. But the target on the radar continued to
gain on him.

It wasn't unusual to change course for the larger fishing vessels and the freighters and tankers that steamed up and down the
New England coast on their business. The vessel on his screen was
now within three miles—still plenty of maneuvering room for a
vessel that size. But Warren decided to play it safe and change
course till he was out of the vessel's way, even if he was disgruntled
at having to do it. He switched off the autopilot and came twenty
degrees to the west, closer to the shoal water. He figured that no
vessel the size of the one on the radar screen would have any reason
to venture into the treacherous shoals and rips.

Warren watched the screen as he steered. The orange glow
swept over his features. His large work-battered hands with their
thick fingers and cracked fingernails rested on the smooth pegs of
the helm. They were relaxed; only Warren's pale blue eyes were
hard and intent.

Occasionally glancing forward into the snow, he saw the
shearwaters and gulls and even Wilson's petrels, sparrowlike birds
that dabbled their toes in the water as they flapped, skittering
away from the *Nancy K.*—to them, an unseen noise that approached out of a density of snow to appear suddenly, cleaving
the water into a white mustache, a waterborne being that roiled
through their roosts and disappeared into the snow as quickly as it
had appeared.

What Warren saw on the screen made him grip the wheel

harder. The vessel was closing faster than ever—had, in fact, seemed to increase its speed.

And it had changed its course along with Warren.

"Goddamn dragger," said Warren out loud. "What's he think he's doing?" But Warren knew that the vessel was too big to be a dragger. And he knew, too, that every time he looked away and then back, the vessel seemed to have grown.

Beyond the pilothouse windows, Warren saw a shifting curtain of snowflakes and luminous blankness, as though he and the *Nancy K.* had somehow been injected, like a ship in a bottle, into the interior of a pearl.

Warren had had run-ins with vessels before, one dragger in particular. On Corsair Canyon many years before, he had shot out the pilothouse windows of a dragger that had hauled up all his gear. He had steamed up to the wallowing boat and crossed its bow, shattering the windows with two blasts of his 10-gauge goose gun.

The thought occurred to him that maybe the vessel was in trouble and needed his help. But why wouldn't it have radioed? Vessels that size would have a backup radio even if the main unit was on the blink.

The unnerving thing about it was that the size of the blip continued to grow. From the size of a kernel of rice, it had widened and lengthened and was now a half inch in diameter, but of no definite shape. Warren now wondered whether his radar was acting up.

Warren tried to raise the vessel on the radio, but he received nothing but static.

He could only imagine that the vessel needed him very badly—or why else would it be pursuing him so relentlessly into foul waters?

He decided to throttle back. The vessel could maneuver alongside and he would find out once and for all what this was all about. He would shout across the water to the skipper to find out what the hell he was up to, scaring him this way and forcing him off course.

He watched the radar as he idled. The vessel—the mass of orange by now—came onward. It showed no sign of slowing. He switched the radar to short-range. The vessel was less than a quarter of a mile away. He grabbed the radio and shouted into it: *"Nancy K., this is the Nancy K. Vessel to my northeast, what the hell are you doing?"*

He watched the target speeding toward him—dead-on on a collision course.

The hell with this, he thought. He jammed the boat into gear and gave it full throttle.

When the vessel changed course after him, the fear that Warren wanted not to think about became a conscious thought: *It does not need help. It is coming after me.*

At full throttle, the *Nancy K.* was still losing ground to the vessel on the radar. On the screen, the mass of orange that the vessel had become was less than five hundred feet behind Warren. Soon the mass would merge with the bloom of orange at the dead center of the radar, the blind spot called sea clutter. Within a certain range—sometimes twenty, maybe fifty, a hundred feet—it was impossible to see what was there.

Then the vessel met and was absorbed by the sea clutter. Warren turned the helm hard to port and ran to the pilothouse door to see whether he could spot rigging, a funnel, anything that might give him a clue of what was chasing him.

Beyond the afterdeck, a wilderness of snow was all he saw.

He stepped to the wheel again and yanked it to starboard. He cut around in a circle, smashing back through his own wake. Suddenly, the vessel emerged from the clutter on the screen and veered around in front to head straight for him.

He spun the wheel again to port, but the vessel turned with him, shadowing him, forcing him away from the shoal water, driving him out to the east and the open ocean as if it were cutting a steer.

What would Gary do if he was here? thought Warren as he watched the vessel paralleling him on the screen. *Would this be happening at all?*

He decided what he had to do. He grabbed the radio to try to raise Don or Lester or Chet and even the Coast Guard, but every channel he tried was sizzling with interference.

The vessel was crowding him again.

Good God, thought Warren. *What is going on here? I can't keep steaming out toward the middle of nowhere. What does this guy want from me?*

There was only one way to find out, and Warren throttled down and clicked the *Nancy K.* into neutral. The boat bobbed up as its own wake swept underneath and then settled into the calm water. Warren went through the pilothouse door to the afterdeck, his heart making his neck feel thick and tight. He leaned against the rail to peer into the snow. He strained to see, strained to hear, but the snow—the snow that his wife had called "pretty" not six hours before—twirled down so hard and with such intensity and such dazzling geometric rhythms that he had to close his eyes. And the mumble of the idling diesel erased any sound.

He looked down at the water, the gray-green water where a few shearwaters paddled. He was waiting for the vessel to emerge. As in fog, when a vessel appeared out of thick snow, it was always a shock to see how close you could be to something so large without seeing it. And now Warren was bracing himself not for a boat that was gingerly feeling its way toward him but for one that was coursing toward him, intentions unknown.

As Warren stared, he realized that had the vessel intended to ram him, it would have done so by now. He peered harder, blinked, and then realized that he was looking directly at something that had been there all along.

It was simply too huge to notice. He had been peering into the snow, expecting to see running lights or the flare of a bow appear high above him.

But what he saw, far enough away so that he could not pick out anything specific, was a darkening behind the wall of snow behind his stern.

The darkening spread outward and upward, an immense darkness like a night cloud. He felt a filament of ice rise inside him. The snow was mesmerizing him. Snow built up on the bill of his cap. He stared at the darkness as it moved toward him, his jaw slackening, his eyes filling with the spiraling, spinning, hypnotizing snow. He slowly reached his hand up and removed the pipe from between his teeth.

The darkening was growing, spreading, rising. Warren wanted to know what it was. He wanted to know what it wanted from him. He called out, "Hello, hello there," his voice slipping off into the snow. He could not take his eyes off the wall of snow and the darkness behind it. Thinking only of snow, he climbed up on the transom. He leaned toward the darkening, squinting, wanting to know.

And then the shearwaters suddenly splattered up off the surface of the water, all of them instantly disappearing into the snow except one.

This shearwater flapped once around the boat. As it came back around the stern by Warren, it veered so close to him that he raised his arm to fend it off. There was a flutter of feathers like shuffled cards. He knocked the snow off the bill of his cap in the process. The bird circled again, gliding by Warren even closer, forcing him to hop back down on the deck. On the bird's next circuit, it flashed so close to Warren that he backed up to the pilot-house door.

And then the cold came over him like a motionless wind, a

presence of cold. The blackness began to fill in behind the snow like ink.

Now the shearwater came straight for him. It flared its slender wings and flapped them in his face, beating at him with its wings and making its frantic beeping call, until he retreated, shaking with cold, into the pilothouse. His breath pumped out in plumes as the dim realization that he had to move, had to do something dawned on him. He hit the throttle with the hand that still gripped his pipe and saw the shearwater flail at the windshield and then fly out ahead of the boat, just within sight. On the radar, the darkness, the vessel—whatever it was—separated from the sea clutter and moved along with the *Nancy K.* Then Warren saw that he was still heading east.

The shearwater flapped back at the window, hovering in front of him. Then it flew off toward the northwest, came back, flew out again, returned.

The vessel drew nearer. It was forcing him to the east again, forcing him out to the deep ocean, beyond the limits of his fuel and endurance. The cold seeped into his consciousness and his thoughts became drugged with the cold. The shearwater flapped in front of him as if to try to jolt him out of this slow descent. Warren looked at the bird flapping, drawing him away from the darkness on the screen. It seemed to be trying to show him something, just as the darkness behind the snow was trying to show him something.

The helm felt stiff but he forced it hard over, bringing the *Nancy K.* around to the northwest. The shearwater glided just ahead, swinging back and forth across the bow of the boat. Warren checked the radar and saw the vessel moving toward him. Then it blended into the sea clutter.

All Warren felt was increasing coldness and the agony of not knowing when the vessel was going to overtake the *Nancy K.*

Warren waited. His hands were clenched on the helm, grinding the pegs. He shut his eyes and then opened them and the shearwater was still there, sailing onward. When, when would it strike? What would it feel like? How long would it be?

Craning his neck, he glanced over his shoulder through the window of the pilothouse door. *Where is it? Why is it so dark behind me? Why is it pursuing me? When will I feel the crash, the crunch, the icy water? When will I die?*

Ahead the shearwater rode on an invisible current. Warren looked at the radar: nothing but sea clutter. Was the darkness hiding in it, using it as camouflage? Still there had been no collision. How many minutes had elapsed? Had he passed the point of collision? The *Nancy K.* steamed onward, homeward. More minutes elapsed. He stepped aft to look out the window. Was it true, was the snow lightening? He came forward and checked the loran and the chart and saw that his position was four hours east of where he believed himself to be.

Ten minutes, a half hour, an hour, and still the shearwater flew with him, and the collision had not yet happened. The tension in his muscles began to drain away and he began to pray, knowing what lay just behind him and what sailed just ahead of him. Before the Great Round Shoal buoys, he took another look through the window and saw that the darkness was gone and the snow had nearly stopped. There was only the white rooster tail of his stern wake, the sea opening behind him, and the retreating clouds.

When he turned forward again, the shearwater was gone.

He passed the two buoys at Great Round Shoal and set a course for Monomoy Point. He steered the boat, feeling drained and weak, his mind still numb. He began to wonder why he had not thought of his family until now. Their faces came to him. He wanted nothing more than to be with them, to see them, to hold them in his arms.

The clouds migrated quickly to the southeast, leaving a winter's after-snow sky. The water became royal blue tinged with the afterglow of the sun, a peach blush separated from the horizon by a long, smooth slate blue cloud shaped like a tilting dish. Above the glow was eggshell and then pale blue, and then navy, and purple, and in the purple the first stars glittering. Now the visibility was limitless. Warren drank in the distances before total darkness set in and he again had to navigate by radar.

When he finally reached the harbor and cleated the last line, he shut off the engine and—silence. No one else was at the harbor. Apparently, no one else had gone out that day.

Warren stood on the deck of his boat. He looked up at the stars. He listened to the roaring in his head—the voice of the engine and of his blood.

He climbed off the boat and walked through the fresh snow to his pickup. He drove home through the snowy town and along the freshly plowed roads. Yellow lights were on in the house as he drove in the driveway, yellow lights that cast blocks of light on the blue snow. He parked and got out, the snow creaking, now calf-high.

He tromped inside to the mudroom, feeling the rush of hot, moist kitchen air as soon as he opened the door.

"Who's there?" called Martha from inside the kitchen. He heard her footsteps on the kitchen floor. He took off his coat and sat on the bench to undo his boots. She appeared in the doorway.

"I thought I heard someone come in. What are you doing back so . . ."

And then she stopped and took in a breath.

"What happened?" she said. "Is everything . . . are you . . ."

Warren got one boot off and held it for a moment and then let it slip out of his hand and fall to the floor. He looked slowly up to her. She knelt before him and laid a hand, still pink and warm from working in the sink, on his shoulder. She took off his cap and stroked his mussed hair.

"I don't know," he said, looking beyond her, over her shoulder. "I just don't know."

That night, they went to bed and lay under the covers. He kept his glasses on. The cat bounded onto the bed and kneaded the spot at their feet, then curled up and went fast asleep. But they didn't sleep. They lay awake under the covers and Martha's hand took his and they stayed awake, listening to the silence surrounding the house.

Eventually she whispered, "Warren, what are you going to do?"

He lay in the warmth under the covers, seeing the stars through the ceiling, seeing the snow, seeing the darkness, seeing the shearwater swinging back and forth before the bow.

He did not know what to do. His life was fishing. His life was the ocean, his boat. He did not know whether he could live that life any longer.

"Warren," she said, turning closer to him. "Warren, you've got to understand something."

He lay still, watching the stars, watching the ceiling.

"It's not over yet," she said. "You can't let it be over."

Is this true, he thought? *Can I go back? Will it happen again? Will it happen forever?*

"You'll go out, Warren, and I'll be with you. We'll go out together, Warren," she said, gripping his hand, her voice louder, its edges quivering. "We'll go out there together tomorrow, you and I. It's ours to hold on to," she said. "We won't let it go."

Warren felt the hard, warm force of her smaller hand in his palm and felt the force of her soul, the force of her life, the force of his life.

And he thought that the mystery of her was not that she was

ever asleep when he thought she was asleep. No, it was something altogether different. The mystery was that every minute of the night, every minute of every day of every year they had been together, she had always been awake.

THE ROPES

It was happening again. It happened every time. Something happened to my dad when we got beyond Monomoy Point and entered the open ocean. Ashore, he was tall, amiable Ed Blackburn. But offshore, something happened to him. It must have been fear. And it was no different this April day with the rising sun going dim behind mottled clouds and an easterly wind sending shivers over the dark gray swells.

I was steering as we passed Monomoy Point, and he stole up behind me and sneaked a look at the loran and the compass.

"What the hell you doing?" he said. "You're way the hell off course. Christ, you'll put us on the beach if you don't watch out." He snapped that not only was it going to cost him fuel but we were also losing valuable time and probably wouldn't make the tide and the fish wouldn't be there when we arrived.

When we began setting the trawl lines, he told Tim, his first mate since before I could remember, that he was miffed at the way he had coiled the gear. He yelled at me that the tubs of gear weren't arranged right on the deck. The flag buoys and anchors were out of place. He even told me I hadn't cut the bait right.

All in all, it was a typical day's fishing with my father. But one thing wasn't typical: It was the last trip I was going to make with him. Even though he didn't know it, I had plans.

After we let the lines soak and we hauled back at the next tide, he grumbled that Tim and I weren't coiling the line back into the tubs correctly. We caught a few scrawny codfish. As I dressed one of the fish between hauls, he shouldered me aside, grabbed the fish, stabbed the knife into it, and said, "Who raised you to be stupid? Do it this way!"

The day wore on. We ate lunch. On the next set, he insisted on baiting every hook of every trawl line. As we steamed over a set, the hooks being snatched out of the tub by the ground line streaming aft, he would hook on the bait and now and then hawk a gob of spit on a hunk of herring, fasten a wild eye on me, and grin and say, "That'll catch one!"

I kept thinking, *I won't ever have to put up with this shit again.*

About the best thing you could say was that the weather wasn't that bad that day. The water itself was still frigid from the winter and the wind was puffing, but it always blew out there. Forty degrees in April was more marrow-numbing than twenty in February. It was like most every other trip I had ever made with my father. He yelled; I worked. And I was supposed to learn.

My father was the only fisherman who knew the holes off Nauset Beach where the halibut lay. He taught me how to find the holes. As we steamed to the spots, he eyeballed the bluffs on the beach and the compass to get his fix on where to set the trawl lines. I had to maintain absolute silence so he wouldn't lose his concentration. Tim could talk, but he never did, because he never did much talking, anyway. Whenever we steamed somewhere and there wasn't any work to be done, Tim dived into the bunk, his watch cap smashed over his face, and snoozed.

My dad made me stay up. "You've got to learn to keep your eyes open, even when you think you can't stand up for one second longer," he said. "It's all part of learning the ropes, boy."

When we fished for halibut, there were always a million volts of tension in the air. One fish could mean a day's pay.

We hadn't caught a halibut on the morning set, and Dad was even more tense than usual when we went to haul back the gear late that afternoon. He handled the helm and the hauler, maneuvering the boat so that the weight of the fish on the hooks wouldn't part the line. Tim coiled the line and hooks back into the tubs. My father kept flicking his eyes from compass to line to hauler to sky and back again. I stood at the rail, gaff at the ready. A good-sized steaker codfish came up and I gaffed it and threw it in the fish box.

"No dogfish today," I said.

"So far," said my father grimly, eyes on the water.

Empty hook after empty hook made its dripping way up from the water. The sun showed orange from behind the thin clouds to the west and the temperature was dropping. All I could think of was getting home, getting dry, getting warm, getting into bed, getting up in the morning, and getting the hell out of there.

But then Dad slowed the hauler and hissed, "We got one, boys."

The tension went tighter than ever. So much could go wrong between seeing the fish and boating it. The hook could give way. The line was taut and could part. The hauler could jam.

Tim stopped coiling and grabbed another gaff to stand ready in case I didn't set my gaff well. I was staring down into the gray-green depths. I still didn't see what my father knew was there. I squinted and strained.

And then, like a figure of a ghost, it showed itself. Rising through the water was a creature of a hundred pounds or more, spinning in the clear, icy water, one moment showing its pure white belly, the next its ink blue back.

I waited, waited, waited for the boat to settle into the trough of a swell and then I swung the gaff with all my might. I felt the hook take meat and I jerked upward, both fists on the long wooden pole. I was already planning to spin it just so on its back in the direction it bent so it would help me bring it aboard, practically swim itself on deck. It would thunder to the deck in a whirl of line and spray. I would try to toss it on its back so it couldn't flip itself back overboard or break something on the boat, like Tim's arm. It would go wild, pounding the deck with its tail, bashing and smashing with its tail and weight. In moments I would be on it with the ball-peen we kept beside the gaff rack, and striking its small head I would hammer it to death.

But planning out my next moves, I got ahead of myself. On this day, the gaff ripped through the flesh. A swell took the boat upward as the fish dived. Tim lunged and took a swipe with his gaff that touched only water. In one second, we were suddenly looking at an empty hook where once we had had a hundred-pound paycheck.

"You stupid son of a bitch!" my father yelled. "What the goddamn hell did you do?"

I looked at him, burning with embarrassment.

"You shut the fuck up!" I blurted. Had I said that? Never before had I crossed him. Through all the years in high school that I had been working for him, I had lived with his crankiness.

But it had been I who had said it. And it had felt good.

"What the hell are you yelling at me for?" I shouted, my voice rising, thinning, spearing. "You're the one steering. You should have seen that wave coming."

I stood at the rail, the gaff in my fist. My yelling seemed to take some of the steam out of him. He stood there breathing hard for a moment and then turned away to look at the compass.

"Goddamn it," he said under his breath, running the hauler as fast as it would go.

It was odd, standing there, having just screamed at my father, who had been screaming at me for so long. It was a kind of victory. It was perfectly timed. I was going my own way. But what I didn't see then was that in another way it was a victory for my father.

★ ★ ★

We got ashore that evening with no halibut and only a few cusk and about two hundred pounds of codfish. My father and I didn't say a word to each other even when we dropped Tim off at his place and he said, "Same time tomorrow?"

That night, after eating, we were sitting around the kitchen table under the bright light. My father read the newspaper, his big hands with the cracked yellow fingernails turning the pages. My mother was scissoring out coupons.

When I said what I had to say, the ions in the air took on a new charge. You could just about hear the static electricity in my father's close-cropped sandy hair. I said I was heading out to Colorado and was going to work construction jobs out there over the summer until the snows came in the fall and then I would start up a snowplowing business.

My parents didn't look at each other. My father kept looking at the paper spread out before him. He licked a finger and turned a page. He smoothed the page with his left hand. Then he said, still without looking at me, "When?"

I suppose I was hoping for their blessing. My father stared at another page and then flipped it before I answered.

"Tomorrow," I said.

There was another long silence and then my mother said, "I thought you were saving for college."

I told her other lies on top of the ones I had told over the past year as I saved up and bought the Bronco and the snowplow. I told her I had kept some aside for the following year. I mentioned about not wanting to go to the community college in Barnstable but a real one off-Cape, about applying somewhere when I was in Colorado and returning in the spring for halibut season and going to college the next fall.

My father folded up his paper and stuck it under his arm. It seemed he suddenly had pressing business elsewhere. He pushed back his chair and stood up. And only then did he turn to me and look at me hard, almost leaning over to bring his long face and hard blue eyes close to mine. Now amiable Ed Blackburn had been transformed into the taskmaster I knew offshore.

And he said, "Have fun."

I remember my mother in the background rising up from the table to do something with the dishes. She must have sensed that something was going to happen—something that had never happened before and that would change things forever. She wanted to create a diversion. Or maybe she wanted to get out of the way.

She must have felt the heat rising inside me. I pushed back my chair and said, "Have fun? What the hell do you mean by that?"

He stopped. He probably didn't expect that I was going to respond for a second time in one day. He looked at me for a moment and then said, "You're running away; that's all you're doing. You're afraid of work. I've had to push you every inch of the way ever since I let you work for me. Now that you're finally worth something, you run off and leave me high and dry." He took his newspaper from underneath his arm and waved it as if at a fly. "So go out to Colorado and have yourself some fun."

By now, I was standing. I was smiling a smile I couldn't stop myself from smiling.

"You've had to push me?" I said. "You're lucky I lasted as long as I did. How the hell do you expect anybody to work for you when you act like Attila the Hun out there all the time? The way you treat Tim, you're lucky he hasn't tried to shove you overboard. Why do you have to be such a bastard all the time?"

He had no answer. He knew he was a bastard offshore, but no one had ever called him one to his face. He stood there under the bright light, staring at me. And then he tucked his newspaper under his other arm and turned and left without a word.

★   ★   ★

The next morning, I set off for Colorado. I found work framing condos in Breckenridge. I loved it. The mountains were spectacular. The aspens were beautiful. The people were easygoing and friendly. Everyone said "Have a nice day."

I was out of there in under two months.

How do you explain why I went back so fast? My mother wrote letters. She gave me the news of the day, but it wasn't that she begged me to return.

I guess it was more that Dad didn't; he could get along fine without me. I had left when I had a chance to begin to make him rely on me as much as I relied on him. But I had left.

So I turned up again one drizzly June morning after driving straight through from Denver with the aid of hitchhikers. I hugged my mom and asked where Dad was. "Down at the harbor, I guess," she said, smiling at me and letting her eyes tear up.

I drove down to the harbor. I got out of the Bronco and shuffled across the dock. All the boats were in their slips. I looked down at the *Mary Ann,* the boat my father had named for my mother so many years ago. Gulls stood on the tops of pilings. The drizzle danced down with the gusty wind. The closest boat to where I was standing was the *Petrel,* a lobster boat. Keith, the skipper, came out on deck and saw me.

"Hey, Tommy," he said. "How you doing?"

He was smoking a cigarette. He had long hair and wasn't much older than I was. He wore a faded blue-jean shirt and paint-and oil-stained khakis, standard fisherman garb. He held an oily monkey wrench in his fist.

"Good," I said. "How's the fishing?"

"You know," he said, smiling that smile that says even if it was terrific, he wouldn't say. "Good days and bad days."

"You seen my old man around?" I said.

"Yeah. Should be up to the shanty. He's getting ready to go tonight, I guess. Supposed to be pretty dirty, but you know your old man."

I smiled. "See you later."

The shanty was beside the harbor. It was a rough-shingled shack with a slanted roof and a wood-plank door. I had spent many hours in that cold, smelly, cramped place: working on gear, shooting the bull with other crewmen, watching my father teach me things I could learn no other place.

I could see a light on inside through the one window with a smashed pane.

Yes, I knew my father, all right. I took hard, long strides toward the shanty, feeling an energy I had never felt before.

I was going back fishing with him. I was ready to learn more. Learning to yell had been only the first lesson.

THE PHEASANT

Marsh was all we could see: 360 degrees of flatness, met only at the distant horizon with a low rim of land to the south and to the north with the creamy waves of dunes along Sandy Neck. The afternoon was waning. The sun tinted the brown grasses orange. To the east, where the marsh met Barnstable Harbor and Cape Cod Bay, flocks of black ducks down from the Arctic flew in a circular holding pattern as they scouted for a place to put in for the night. From their height, they had us in their sights, even though we were a good three miles distant: My older brother Steve and I were hunting in the epicenter of the expanse of low grass that the November frosts had clipped to ankle height. The ducks had no intention of flying near us. The only place to take cover, to hide from sharp duck eyes, was in the ditches, the tributaries of the tidal river, which at high tide were filled to the brim with salt water and at low tide offered steep slimy banks twelve feet high pocked with hermit crab holes. At the bottom of these drained creeks lay quicksand and mucky glurp the color of petroleum that ate men whole, or at the least sucked rubber boots off hunters' legs as a reminder of a never-sated appetite.

The ground underfoot quaked with each step. To the ducks, we were two tiny upright figures carrying sticks that dealt death; to ourselves, we were two insignificant forms in a shivering sea of grasses and sky.

"Let's check the ditches on the way back," said Steve. As much as you tried to keep your eyes open for ducks on the move, it was impossible in so large an area to spot every motion. While you kept your eyes on a pair of mergansers or buffleheads or goldeneyes coming toward you from the south, a few black ducks or mallards could slip into hiding in a ditch behind you.

My father had taught my brother and me to hunt. In the rolling hedgerow fields of southeastern Pennsylvania, the three of us had hunted for pheasant, quail, and woodcock. Before I was old enough to handle a shotgun, I tagged along, a human bird dog. One Christmas, we went out in a snowstorm to try out Steve's new 12-gauge double-barrel shotgun. My big present was a genuine coonskin cap that was just like my hero's, Daniel Boone. Dad and Steve had their orange hunting hats on. I wore my coonskin cap. Strangely, we left before Mom and my little sister, Liz, had finished opening their presents. I was eight and I wasn't sure what was going on, but Dad was angry about something and Steve was angry about something and they weren't saying anything to each other. Sitting together in the front of the station wagon, they kept a strange, cold silence. My brother probably didn't want to sit with my dad, but he wasn't about to give up his older brother's right to sit up front.

We drove along the deserted country roads through the heavy snow to a farm whose owner was a friend of Dad's. We trudged away from the barn and the farmhouse and headed up a hill that was covered with brambles. The going was rough in the deep snow. But I was having a fine time, at least when I forgot that something was wrong with my brother and father. Had something happened back at the house? Why was it that Mom had spent so much time in the kitchen instead of by the tree with the rest of us? Was she crying because she was happy, the way she always did on Christmases before?

We fanned out, Dad off to the left, Steve to the right, I in the middle and behind. I remember the snow falling in a slant in thick uniform flakes that fell so hard and fast, it made you lean forward off balance. I was dizzy with delight, for the storm meant tobogganing and snow forts and snowshoeing and snowball fights. I even let myself fall facedown into the snow for the sheer fun of it. Dad didn't look. My brother shook his head and curled his upper lip.

We reached the brow of the hill. The hill sloped into corn stubble. Beyond that, nothing was visible but the suggestion of a hedgerow and beyond that a blank backdrop of snow.

When the pheasant, a ring-necked cock bird, flushed from the bramble patch, I didn't see it; I only heard it. The bramble patch was between Dad and Steve. The bird, as richly colored as an Oriental rug, struggled out from the brambles, sending up a sound like a fan gone haywire. The sound was muffled by the blizzard. Chunks of snow flew as the bird beat its short wings to gain height. My brother wheeled, raised his shotgun, and fired. I saw the gun kick and the smoke blow out the muzzle before I heard the gun fire.

At the firing of my brother's gun, my father dropped down as though he had stepped in a hole with no bottom.

At exactly the same time, the bird flinched. Then it set its wings, coasted down the other side of the hill, and vanished into a stand of locust that was draped with jungles of snow-covered thickets.

My father was upright again in an instant, as though he had hit a trampoline. In four strides, he was over to Steve. Steve stood absolutely still. As Dad approached, he lowered his gun. My father reached out and grabbed the barrel of Steve's gun.

"Give it to me!" he yelled. "You son of a bitch, give it to me!"

They pulled the gun back and forth, back and forth, a tug-of-war. A shell must have still been in the right chamber, since Steve had fired just once. I held my breath. Their breath blew out.

"Who do you think you are?" yelled my brother, his voice cracking. "Why did you do that to her?"

"Give me the gun," said my father, no longer yelling. "Give me the gun."

My brother gave an almighty yank and twisted the gun out of my father's grip. My father staggered backward as Steve raised the gun and fired into the air. The snow made the sound go *whump*.

Then Steve headed back down the hill toward the farm in great long strides, not once looking back as my father yelled "Get back here!" after him.

We watched Steve get smaller and smaller and dimmer and dimmer until he almost disappeared in the snow. From the hill you could make out the ghostly shapes of the farm buildings. Steve's figure made a small silhouette, his gun over his shoulder, as he reached the bottom of the hill and headed toward the buildings.

All I could hear was the whisper of snow against my canvas hunting coat. My father's breath came slower and slower.

Without looking at me, he said, "Well shit," and struck off along the ridge faster than I could ever walk, even though I tried for half a mile or so, struggling and once falling flat in the cold steely snow so hard that tears came to my eyes. He kept going. That was enough for me. I decided to double back to do what I had been brought along to do: track the bird. I went back to the bramble patch and got my bearings. I walked down the hill and entered the woods where I figured the bird had gone in.

After casting around for a bit, wading around in the snow and undergrowth, overhanging branches brushing the snow off my coonskin cap, I found a feather that hadn't yet been covered by snow. Farther along I spotted a drop of ruby blood on the snow. I pushed through the thicket, the quiet surrounding me. All I could hear was the whisper of the snow. The undergrowth grew more dense. I found another feather and more drops of blood. At one point, I heard a muffled gunshot from far away and froze in my tracks, my heart trebling in speed. It came from the direction my father had gone. Had he flushed another bird?

I waited until my heart evened out to crawl through the honeysuckle and grape vines after the bird. I came into what seemed a small, protected room where only a filtering of snow penetrated the tangle of branches and dead leaves overhead. Inside this pocket was peace. I crawled in and listened. It was like a private dwelling, like being underground. Drawing my knees up, I nestled my coonskin cap down until the fur tickled the tops of my cold ears. I listened. Only the snow made sound: whisper, whisper, whisper. I waited. I listened. I lay down on my back and let the tiny downy snowflakes drift onto my face. I turned my face away when the snow tickled my nose.

After I had turned my head, it took a minute to see what I was looking at, a foot away from my face. Out of the leaves and branches and vines and grasses beside me that formed a natural wall materialized the pheasant. The bird sat motionless in the midst of this camouflage. I saw its obsidian eye, its beak as yellow as a kernel of corn. It blinked. Out of one nostril on the beak, a tiny bead of blood gathered. I stayed as motionless as the bird. I waited. The bird blinked again. I had been taught to snap the neck of winged birds so they wouldn't suffer long. But I couldn't reach out and take the bird by its neck and twist it and feel its struggle into death.

I watched it. Its lizardy eyelids were drooping. Gradually, I sent my hand out, as softly and imperceptibly as I could manage. My gloved hand reached its feathers and I let it descend as soft as air. I put more and more pressure on the bird's back and slowly brought my other hand around, all the time keeping my eyes on its eyes. It gave one flutter as I drew it toward me, but by this time I had its wings under my gloved hands. I cradled the bird with one arm and unbuttoned my coat with the other hand. I wrapped my coat around the bird as I held it against my sweater. I could feel it quivering, but slowly the quivering lessened. I spoke to it in low tones. A bead of blood, tear-shaped, slid off its beak and hit the canvas of my coat, instantly turning into a spot of black. The snow filtered down through the branches. I lay on my side with the pheasant inside my coat, only its head sticking out, its body quieting, and the snow kept falling.

We picked our way across the marsh, heading in the direction of the long sweep of low dunes. Cradling his shotgun, Steve stayed out to my left and a few feet ahead. Though we wore canvas hunting coats and hip boots, the day had been relatively mild for the middle of November. But a change was coming. From the setting sun arching over our sky to the eastern horizon spread a plume of cirrus. The light was going from orange to brassy. Way over by the dunes, I could see a flock of starlings forming and reforming like a swarm of locusts. From where we were, the flock looked like a black airborne amoeba, a single entity, elongating one minute, fluttering in a barrel roll the next, shifting, rising, swooping. At times, the flock settled into the grass and disappeared. On some mysterious cue, the flock would rise again into the air.

We came to the lip of one of the kettle ponds in the middle of the marsh. These ponds contained crystalline water but went deep into the ground in a shape like a test tube, so, as clear and cobalt as they looked on the surface, you usually couldn't see to their bottoms. Steve came over and peered into its depths with me.

"Next stop, China," he said.

We skirted the kettle pond, walking carefully.

Steve said, "We should do this more often."

"I know," I said. "It's been too long."

"I can't believe we haven't hunted together since, what was it, that time we hunted with your buddy Carl and his dad?"

I laughed. "We wore those camouflage outfits that his dad made. How long ago was that, fifteen years?"

He laughed, too.

"At least. We looked like Visigoths from the steppes."

"He made those vests out of burlap bags. Skirts, too."

"The ducks didn't fall for it. I don't think we got a shot off all day."

"Some things never change."

We were nearing the edge of the marsh. The flock of starlings was still performing its aerobatics. The flock would expand and then coalesce, turn into a banner one minute and a bubble the next. We were close enough to hear the whir of wings.

It was a happy sensation to be heading home after hunting since dawn, even though we were returning empty-handed. My hunting days were infrequent at best. I lived in a distant city, returning to the place that long ago my mother had brought Steve, my sister, and me only when the urge to see old friends and feel old muscles overwhelmed me.

It was less than a year after the Christmas when my brother narrowly missed shooting my father that my family dispersed. My brother went away to boarding school; my mother, my sister, and I moved to Cape Cod. Vacations and summers, Steve spent with us. We hunted in the marshes and woods whenever he was around in season. My father moved far away, to Los Angeles. I didn't see him much after that. Once, twice, he sent me plane tickets. But I had seen him less and less over the years.

★   ★   ★

Now my brother worked for an oil company and had graying temples. My sister, mother, and I used to get together for Christmas at my mother's place on Cape Cod, but soon our own families became an excuse that we, or at least I, had been hunting for: When we got together, there was an undercurrent of sadness, a kind of yearly mourning for a family that had died long ago. I was relieved when the wake was finally over.

Texaco sent my brother all over the world. He had an apartment in London, but he was never there. The first year he took us up on our invitation to come for Christmas at our house, he told my wife that it was the first time he felt he was having a Christmas that was what Christmas was supposed to be—ever. And he had given me a look.

From then on, he came to Christmas at our place, if he could manage it, and once he even flew in on Christmas day from Aberdeen, bearing kilts for the kids. He usually flew off the next day for another distant destination.

But we hadn't had a chance to go hunting together since he had graduated from college, until now, in November, when he stopped over on his way from London to Port Arthur.

There were two more big ditches to jump. The first one, we crossed easily. The last one, even closer to the dunes, we had to scout around to find a place to cross. It was too wide to jump and too treacherous to pass through. Steve struck off along its edge, saying over his shoulder, "Too far to jump for old farts like us."

As he walked away, I looked in the opposite direction to see whether the ditch was any narrower. When I looked back, two black ducks erupted from down in the ditch. They flew up between us.

"Ducks!" I said, snapping my shotgun to my shoulder and

aiming at the lead duck, which was heading dead away from me at no higher than shoulder level.

Something made me hesitate. I followed the duck down the barrel, drawing a bead, and one second later the duck crossed over Steve's head. He whirled and fired, dropping the first duck, and then shot at the other, which banked and flew off quacking. Steve looked at me. I still held my gun where I would have shot: aimed directly at his head, not twenty paces away from me.

I lowered my gun and went over to him as he worked his way halfway down into the ditch to collect his duck.

"I almost got you," I said. Patches of my skin ran in chills. I was sweating. I was queasy. I pictured Steve's face, peppered with blood or half gone. What if it had happened?

He picked up the duck by its legs. The bird's wings lolled open, showing their lighter undersides. The feet were bright reddish orange, almost glowing in the dying light.

"What?" he said. "Naw you didn't. You *should've* shot. We'd have two now instead of one. I had a better shot at the other one, anyway."

"If I'd pulled the trigger . . ." I said.

"Give me a hand," he said, tossing the duck onto safe ground. "The muck's getting me."

I reached out my hand and he gripped my forearm. Up he came, his gun held out to one side, the muck letting go of his boots with a popping snort.

The starlings were still whirring as we stepped onto the sand road and walked toward the pickup truck. Unloading my shotgun, I held the two shotgun shells in my hand. They were as heavy as two rolls of quarters.

The door to the truck squeaked as I opened it. I sat down, my legs heavy, tired, unsteady. I looked out over the marsh, the sky now only a faint pewtery glow. I rolled the shells in my palm.

Steve said, "You okay?"

I looked at him, the immense marsh his backdrop. I tried to read in his eyes a message that would burn through the clouds of the past, but if there was one, I couldn't find it.

"You okay?" he said again.

And I wished I could have held the pheasant I had cradled in my coat long ago and brought it back to life.

N O O N

Arthur Shay backed the boat into the slip, shut off the engine and the running lights, and walked aft to make sure his crewmen had tied the lines right. He had been out for three days with a crew of two to help him haul the longlines. By the time the crew had unloaded the fish, about three thousand pounds of cod, the ice truck showed up, and the crew stowed a load of ice in the fish box. Arthur Shay was planning to leave the next morning on another three-day trip. He was making money, and back-to-back trips did not wear him down so badly when he was making money.

He drove home. It was about ten o'clock at night. He pulled into the sand driveway and was surprised to see that his wife's pickup truck wasn't there. Clare always took the pickup truck when he went offshore because it was the better vehicle, his being an old Rambler. He got out of the old car and stood in the driveway admiring the scent of the roses on the picket fence out front and the smells of the land, the crickets in the woods, the stars above that weren't as sharp as they were offshore but somehow softer, friendlier. He saw headlights coming up the road. They swept across the trees and then across his body. The pickup pulled in beside the Rambler. His wife sat for a long moment in the pickup with the motor idling, so long that he turned and went down the driveway to see whether there was something wrong.

There was. She was in tears. She was a wreck. This was his wife of fifty years and he had never seen her so emotional. He reached his hands out to her and she brushed them away and he said, "What's the matter?" At first she didn't look at him, but then she stared hard at him with fire-red–rimmed eyes.

"You're what's the matter. I think I'm in love with someone else and have been for a year and I can't stand it anymore. I can't live this way."

He laughed. He chuckled. He laughed and the stars were still above him though they were tilting away from him and he said, "What?"

She said, "You heard me. You heard me. *You heard me!*" And she began sobbing.

He felt his hands on her arm and for some reason he could do nothing but chuckle. He felt his hands on her arm and on her knee and he said, "This can't be true."

But he already believed it. He could believe anything. He felt as if someone could walk up to him and say the earth was square and he would believe it, that he could believe anything.

She said, "You're hurting me, Art. Let me go."

"Who?" he said. "Who is it?"

"Let go of me, Art," she said, and he stopped chuckling, but he was smiling and he knew it because his teeth were dry and his lips were stuck to his dry teeth. And she said, "Tom. It's Tom. I'm in love with Tom."

"Tom," he said. He knew it was true, not because of any look in her eye but because this wasn't his wife anymore. But when had he let his wife vanish? A swift succession of images lashed through his mind: Pensacola during the war, and Clare outside the church with the palmettos in the sunbaked yard; on the Cape after the war, and Clare waving from the beach parking lot as he headed offshore;

Clare and the girls in white going to Mass as he drove in the driveway exhausted and reeking of fish after a week-long trip; the long years of seeing each other only in passing.

He looked at her, but he didn't know this woman with the wild, curly gray hair and the red-rimmed gray eyes that had once entranced him. Her white-knuckled hands still gripped the steering wheel. She was no longer looking hard at him, but at someplace else. The thought hit him: *If she looks, I can change everything.* But she didn't look.

"Tom Sanderson," he said. His wife still did not look at him.

Arthur Shay let go of his wife and went into the house and got the .45 automatic he had kept since his Navy days in the Pacific. He came back out, passing his wife. This time, she looked.

"Where are you goin' with that?" she said.

He did not say another word. He got into the pickup and backed out and sped off, his mind a blank. He stared dead ahead. The road, lighted by his headlights, raced toward him and at the last moment poured underneath the hood of the pickup. He leaned forward, the steering wheel touching his chest. Trees flashed by along the sandy road bank. When he pulled to a stop on the crushed-shell driveway of Tom Sanderson's beautiful house ("My pile of shingles," Tom Sanderson had once joked), the blankness had given way to sobbing, a gagging, choking sob that was harsher than his wife's. He kicked at the side door of the house. It wouldn't give way, but the kicking stopped his sobs. He tried the knob and the door opened. Then he took the stairs four at a time and called out, *"Sanderson!"*

From the living room, where he and Clare and Tom had played euchre and drunk highballs many a night, he saw Tom Sanderson through the picture window. He stood down on the dock in the floodlights tying or untying a line to the skiff. Arthur ran back down the stairs and sprinted across the slope, his moccasins getting wet in the dew. He hit the dock and pounded down it and

Tom was rising up and his eyes were opening wide and his hands were coming out and Arthur punched the muzzle of the pistol against Tom's chest and said, "You're going to die."

Tom Sanderson's mouth moved, but no words came forward at first. And then he—he, the man who called himself his friend, a man who had also served in the Navy in the Pacific during the war, a kindred soul; he, this lanky white-haired gent—lowered the lids on eyes Arthur Shay knew to be sky blue and said, "She doesn't love you. She loves me."

At that moment, there was a screeching of Rambler brakes back up at the driveway and both men looked. The next thing Arthur knew, he was flying through the air and plunging into dark water. He surfaced sputtering and turned around. Gasping, he tried to raise the gun, but suddenly Clare was there in front of Tom. Arthur was treading water and saying nothing, but he was coughing salt water. He swam to shore and trudged up the sand, dripping like a retriever. He had lost one shoe. Clare stood between him and Tom. Arthur went slogging up the slope over the grass, the lights glaring down at him, and when he reached the house, he pitched the pistol at the picture window as hard as he could, but it did not break it; it bounced off into a bed of roses.

He drove the pickup down to the supermarket and bought enough groceries to last a week offshore. The people he passed in the aisles either gave him a funny look or wouldn't look at him at all. His clothes still sopping, wearing only one shoe that creaked with salt water, he limped around the store behind his cart, leaving wet footprints. Then he drove to the harbor and fished out the bottle of Old Mr. Boston rum he stowed under the stove in the galley and later passed out in a bunk below.

The morning after was clear and sunny, a perfect summer day. He lay on the bunk of his boat, looking at butterflies of reflected sunlight on the ceiling.

"She doesn't love you," Tom Sanderson had said. "She loves me."

He sat up and patted the top pocket of his denim shirt, which was still damp. He found his Camels. They, too, were soggy, but he managed to extract one and light it with the Zippo lighter that he had saved from his Navy days, one that opened with a pleasing metal-against-metal scratch and that lighted the first time every time, even after a dousing such as last night's. The first drag started him off coughing. Alternately coughing and sucking in and blowing out cigarette smoke, he stood and grabbed his khakis, which were lying on the other bunk, and pulled them on over his boxer shorts. Not too wet. Then he went topside in his bare feet and into the pilothouse to brew coffee.

Through the windows of the pilothouse, he saw the freshly painted summer boats all riding on their moorings on the blue water, their reflections jiggling beside them; the little fleet of sailing dinghies with the kids in orange life preservers racing in the outer harbor; the white-trimmed buildings of the boat works; the pennants waving breezily from the yacht club's mast; the bright green grasses growing in the shallows and the pines on the banks against the washed blue sky; and the soaring gulls and diving terns. He surveyed it all and thought, *What has happened to me?*

He needed coffee in a bad way and with quaking hands and banging head he lighted the stove with his lighter and set the coffee brewing. He lighted another cigarette and tried to think about what he should do. Surely Tom Sanderson would have called the police to press charges; surely he would be pursued; surely he would end up not only losing his wife to a man who had called himself his friend but also losing his freedom, losing his boat and his livelihood. But the police would have been here by now.

And what was this other feeling, this curious feeling, this lightness? The outskirts of a hangover, the remnants of drunkenness ready to collapse into agony? It seemed that the one moment of rage had purged him. He felt light. And he felt an urge to be moving, to be doing something. What was he waiting for?

He poured himself a mug of coffee and rubbed his hand over his close-cropped hair. It was curious, this feeling: It was a feeling of relief.

He saw that his wife of fifty years was a woman who could no longer stand living the way she lived. The years must have been slow, grinding torture. He had extinguished a spark that Tom Sanderson had rekindled. Through the years, she was a woman who was very definite about what mattered: her children, her house, her vegetable garden. She must have settled it with herself long ago that having a husband who was gone all the time was something that was in the scheme of things for her. But she had decided that it was time to shift the scheme.

He set his coffee mug on the bulkhead above the wheel and hit the starter on the engine. The diesel started up and idled in its whiskey tenor. Arthur opened a locker, found an old pair of sneakers, and put them on without socks. Then he went forward and released the bowline and spring line, came aft and cast off the stern line, then stepped back into the pilothouse and put her into gear.

He was suddenly infected with an overwhelming urge to go, to leave, to run away, to go as fast and as far away as possible. He cleared the breakwater that led into the outer harbor. The sunlight shattered on the Sound in a million shards and he pushed the throttle higher. A Windsurfer knifed by him on the smooth water and waved and Arthur did not wave back but stepped to the door and looked aft at the shoreline and the parking lot at the beach. There were a few cars there, their windshields reflecting the sun, but never again would his wife tell him in her soft Floridian accent to be careful now, nor would she be sitting there waving the way she had for decades—waving falsely, waving for what?

The kids had grown up and left and there were only chores and a bigger garden in the back acre for her. Still he went offshore, many times having to go farther and stay longer in order to bring home half of what he had caught before. He knew he would never make enough to retire. But Clare seemed not to mind or at least to be resigned to it, because it was never a subject of conversation, let alone contention. She went about her business ashore. They treated each other like workers on different shifts.

He brought the throttle up to cruising speed, passing day sailors and watching the mirage of Monomoy Island to the southeast gradually take on clarity and substance. Visibility was limited only by the curve of the earth. The sea was bright blue, the sky pale blue, the light white. Already the dunes on Monomoy looked larger than reality. He set his usual course for the Point and poured himself another mug of coffee, the boat riding stiff and steady across the water.

All he wanted to do was steam on this steady course. It was the kind of day that everything at noon would seem to be a negative, so bright and clear as to be drained of color. The colors would be vibrant when the sun got lower, as they were now, in the morning, as the sun climbed, but at noon the sun would bleach the sky and force the pupils so tight that color would be secondary to light and shadow.

Behind him, the Cape was breaking up into miragelike islands. Soon it would disappear altogether, he would round the point, steer into the first Atlantic swells, and head into the open ocean. Where would he go? He could stay far from land, out on the continental shelf. Or he could steam for Nova Scotia.

He thought, *I can do anything I want.*

As he neared the Point and the empty beaches of Monomoy, he changed course and throttled down. He would bring the boat into the shallows along the beach, take her into a cove, stop for a minute and think. Yes, he needed to think. He would anchor up, cook some breakfast, and think.

Minutes after changing course, the bottom was visible. The island was still two miles off, but shallow flats extended around it from the point to where Monomoy reached the Cape near Stage Harbor. He idled along, looking down through the clear pale green water at the sandy bottom and the clumps of weed like dark gardens and the bright white seashells.

When he got within a hundred yards of the beach at a depth of about ten feet, he put the boat into neutral and went below to get the anchor out of the forepeak. He dragged the anchor topside to the bow and dropped it over, watched it descend and hit bottom in a little puff of sand. He could see its flukes dig in and bury themselves in the sand. He went back into the pilothouse and did something he would rarely do offshore: He shut down the engine. The silence was amazing, huge and freeing, and in it came many sounds from many directions. He heard gulls over on the island, the lap of waves against the hull of the boat, a few squeaks and creaks of the boat herself as she pulled at the anchor line, the gentle wash of the waves on the beach ahead of him.

From the icebox, he took out eggs and bacon and got the bacon frying and then cracked two eggs and fried them in the bacon grease. Then he took out two pieces of raisin bread and dropped them for a minute beside the eggs in the frying pan. Then he broke the yolks of the eggs, took the slices of bread out, and laid them on the counter. He piled on the bacon and the eggs on the bread and made a sandwich. Then he ripped a piece of paper towel off the roll and took his sandwich out on the afterdeck in the sunshine. He faced the sun and ate.

When he was finished, he took off his still-damp shirt and lighted a cigarette and lay back on the fish box. The sun had climbed high and a line of white puffy clouds along the northern horizon showed where the Cape was even though land wasn't visible. Across the water, sunlight glinted off a few boats' windshields, but no boat was within two miles of him. He dozed off and then woke thinking a hornet was stinging his lips and he spat out the burned-down butt. He was sweating. He looked around and, seeing no boats, stripped down to his boxer shorts. He lay back down and closed his eyes against the sun.

When Arthur Shay woke, he pushed himself up on one elbow and scanned the horizon. How long had he been asleep? Sweat was trickling down his chest. He hopped off the fish box and went forward. He looked down at the anchor line rubbing in its chock and angling into the water. He had heard of sailors jumping overboard for a dip and watching their boats suddenly move away from them, leaving them stranded, treading water until they could tread no more.

He stripped off his boxer shorts and climbed out on the pulpit and dived, his body with its hard old muscles flexed belying the fact that it had spent nearly seventy years on the earth. It was a body that could still fit into his dress whites. He hit the water and felt liquid ice surround him. He swam down, down, until he touched the soft sand on the bottom. He opened his eyes and saw the anchor and the anchor line. He swam underwater toward it, grabbed it, and pulled himself hand over hand to the surface. He gasped as he surfaced and clung to the anchor line, the sun flashing around him on the water.

God, how wonderful this feels, he thought, diamonds of water dripping from his head. And he wondered how long it had been since he had last gone swimming, having gained the fisherman's superstition about jinxing yourself by swimming in the same water you fish in. Then he pushed away from the anchor line and swam the breaststroke the hundred yards over the shallows to the beach. He emerged dripping, his weathered skin cold and taut, his arms and neck burned brown, the rest of his body pale. His eyes burned with salt. He waded the last few yards, bait fish tickling against his feet and light reticulating the clear water in crazy patterns. He walked up on the hot sand of the beach, sending a storm of sea gulls into the air ahead of him. His wet feet wore slippers of sand. He crossed the sand to a bluff and climbed up it and hunkered down on it over his shadow. The sun baked his body.

He crouched there in the sand and the sharp eelgrass, dripping, his forearms resting on his knees, a naked man with the salt water dripping off his fingertips and drying on his back, looking across the water at his boat as it rode to anchor. At this hour, noon, the boat was in silhouette, a black mirage amid the white sparkles on the water.

Then he rose and turned in the other direction. He dogtrotted across the spine of the skinny island and paused at the crest of the dune to scan the open Atlantic. Rollers rising out of a navy blue sea crashed along the miles of beaches. He sprinted for them, running hell-bent downhill, flushing flights of herring gulls from their roosts into the air. He hit the wash of the surf without even slowing and plowed into icy water. He swam for a big comber that was meeting shore after its immense journey and felt the power of it lift him, carry him, propel him back toward the beach. He rode it, beginning to laugh, rode it until the wave broke and he was tossed and spun and cartwheeled beneath the surface. He felt the pebbles and the sand scrape his thighs and chest and the suds race back around his body. He lay on his belly on the slant of the beach. He heard the pebbles clatter as the water retreated.

He lay in the sun, spitting and laughing, at first with exhilaration, then suddenly crying as though he had been crying all along and never planned to stop. He gasped for air as another wave crashed over him. The foam rushed back to the sea. Another wave crashed over him.

The gulls, too recently spooked to be sure about settling back onto their island, flapped in the sky over their shadows and eyed the figure of the man lying belly-down in the surf.

—◯—

C A W

From way across the field, you could see Joe Peavey sitting in the tree. He perched on one of the uppermost branches of a lightning-struck pine that stood alone at the edge of the rows of corn stubble. Woods bordered the field, mostly maple and oak and a few birches and some pines. Only one part of the tree he sat in was alive—a big shock of bristly green needles that pointed off to one side like the horn of an anvil. The rest of the tree was bare and the color of bones with only a few patches of scabby bark.

From that distance, he looked like a scrap of blown-away kite that had gotten snagged on the limb.

I crossed the field in the dying light. The corn stubble, tinted orange from the sun as it sank, ran in ranks to the woods. The orange light bathed the trees in the woods and glowed in the sky near the sun.

"Joe," I said, standing beneath him. This close, I had to crane my neck to see him. He had climbed very high up.

"Hello there, Cook, my friend," he said. "It's kind of you to come by."

"Don't mention it," I said. "The boys at the harbor said you've been out here for a couple of days. Couldn't drag you down with a grappling iron." From away in the deeper woods, crows called. I knew him well enough not to push him. He'd tell me himself by and by why he had climbed the tree, though the boys at the harbor knew and had told me.

"You're awfully high up there," I said, stepping backward to get a better view. "Night's coming on."

The light shifted a shade, a deeper, richer orange, so that every blade of the grass growing in a patch around the base of the tree caught the light and glowed copper.

"This'll be my third night up here," he said. I saw him looking westerly. "They brought food and water, but I told them they were wasting their time." From his vantage point, he could see the lumpy hills running to the sea.

"Night or not, I'll still be up here."

He was long and gaunt, handsome like a hawk, and he crouched there like a young bird of prey trying to get up the nerve to take its first flight. He bent and stretched his long legs and worked his free arm in its shoulder socket. He squatted on his haunches, not dangling his legs, and held on to the trunk with one long hand, the fingers hooked in a hole drilled by a woodpecker or flicker.

"I suppose you know it's Faye," he said finally, still looking outward, away to the far hills and the plate of the sea.

"Ah, Joe," I said. "You know about Faye. You shouldn't be troubling yourself over her. She's given you enough trouble for one lifetime. She's given us both enough trouble for both our lifetimes."

Over the field came a flock of starlings shifting and changing its shape like an aerial kaleidoscope. A breeze sneaked around us, whispering in the grass.

"Well," he said. "I'm not coming down. I'm not coming down until she comes out here and tells me she loves me.

"Which she does," he added.

My shadow now stretched three quarters of the way across the field. I shoved my hands into my coat pockets.

"You must be starving," I said. "Come on down. I'll buy you a burger and a beer."

"You're not listening to me, Cook, my friend." He almost whispered now, and the night breeze whispered in the orange grass.

"I'm not coming down," he said, "till she comes out here and tells me she loves me."

I was afraid he was telling the truth. He had let Faye do to him what she had done to me. We had chosen to hear her siren's murmur and we had sailed toward it.

"Cook, I need your help," he whispered. "Go talk to her. She listens to you."

I almost laughed at that.

"Faye listen to me? When I see her around town, she looks through me. She doesn't even look at me and then look away. She doesn't see me."

He whispered fiercely.

"Go talk to her, Cook. Tell her I want to talk to her. Tell her I'm not coming down until she tells me she loves me."

"Hell, Joe, she wouldn't even open her door if I were to hammer on it."

"She will. She knows I'm here. Talk to her."

"You know where to find me," he said. His profile hunched against the sky, a hawk with no wings to soar on.

I knew he would not be swayed because a man in love with someone who isn't in love with him cannot afford to be swayed or he loses everything. He's got to keep trying. He's got to keep trying even though he cannot know what he must change in order to be loved. Faye was a force unto herself. Joe was dealing with the wind. He was hoping to turn night into day. He was spellbound by her. I was his last hope.

At the edge of the field, I turned and looked back, hoping that he might have decided that it was time to give it up and so had climbed down to follow me for a ride back home. He would be silent and sulk in his beer, then go to his place and lie down and look at the ceiling and feel like the last leaf on a tree. Gradually he would know it was over. He would go on with his life, emptier, freer, sadder, happier.

But I squinted down the rows of stubble to the far side of the field and the woods. I could see him in the dimming light: like windborne litter caught in the tree.

The walk back through the woods to my car and the drive back to town took less than a half hour. I got to Faye's cottage in starlight. In my car's headlights, leaves leapfrogged across the lane leading to her cottage and there was a shivering drift of them in front of her door. Warm yellow light poured out of the windows and I could smell wood smoke. But I knew better than to think this place inviting. Inside lived a woman who could make fire burn cold.

Almost as soon as I knocked, the door opened.

"Come in, Cook," she said. "Don't stand out there in the dark."

I hadn't expected pleasantness. What had once been between us wasn't love because I believe that love is something that has a life of its own, something that cannot die no matter how hard two people try to make it die. Even one tenacious soul can keep it alive.

What had been between us was more of a spell, a trance, and it ended strangely because it wasn't the trance that ended but nearly my life. Surely my life as I had lived it was dead. Even now, stepping into the cottage once again, I could not be certain the spell had evaporated.

The cottage was furnished simply: a sofa, a worn oriental rug, antique fireplace implements, a seascape or two on the walls, comfy chairs. Faye kept the books for a number of local businesses, among them a gas station, a real estate agency, a fish market, and several antique stores. She lived the life so typical among year-round residents of our little town on Cape Cod, where there aren't enough livings to go around and to survive you must be a jack-of-all-trades. Faye got by. But to see her as the sum of her jobs was to miss the essence of this woman, this force, this high wind on a baleful night.

She motioned to the sofa, but I kept standing, moving over to the fireplace, where a high fire was burning, snapping and cracking. She was a tall woman whose high cheeks had flush spots like blooms on them, as though she had always just stepped in from a walk in the woods. She had indigo eyes and black hair, skin as white as daisy petals. When she was enraged, she could curse worse than the fishermen I knew, the boys at the harbor.

But she lived alone and saw no one, and the reason, I believed, was that her own power over men frightened her the way a clairvoyant might fear his own powers to see into others' lives, damned to glimpse the secret chambers of humanity. She had been blessed with the power or cursed with it. But something else occurred to me. Had she chosen not to use her power because she thought it wasn't worth using?

Years ago, I had seen her walking alone on the beach and I imagined myself flying over the water with her, hand in hand, skimming the crests of oceanic swells, and I prayed for the courage to talk to her. I had heard from the boys at the harbor, who had seen or heard of her first, that she was beautiful and untouchable, like a furious yet stunning falcon. I asked her out.

In less than a week, I was spending every night with her. In less than a month, I was living in her cottage. In less than two months, I was out of work. In less than a year of being with her, I was a certified drunk living in a old duck-hunting camp without light or heat at the far end of Hawk's Nest Pond, not far from the field where Joe was now perched, perhaps muttering to himself, weakening physically as Faye's spell solidified around him like a cooling mold of iron.

And where was Faye during my demise? One moment, I was absorbed by Faye. I slipped with her into a different sea. She had drawn me in and let me dwell within her. In the deep, we floated together, and time did not pass. The next moment, she finned away, shattering the spell, marooning me on cold, hard rock.

I had traded one intoxication for another. I wasn't sure when I left her cottage and burrowed into the hunting camp. I believed I had become a crow and was living with the gangs of crows that roam the woods and fields. I would stand out in the woods, watching the flocks up in the treetops, and imitate their calls: the caw-caw warning cry; the call they use to express amusement, a rattling sound like a nut shaken in a wooden box; the nasal sneer they use to razz each other and to mock humans and other land-imprisoned animals. Once, after throwing up blood and writhing in pain for three days, I found myself at a doctor's. The medico told me I had liver damage and would surely return to the earth, six feet of it, should I continue my life as a crow. Joe dragged me out of the cabin one night when he showed up and found me sprawled on the floor unconscious. I lived at his house until I shed my crowness and became a whole man again and could work and feed myself and stay off the sauce.

While I was recovering from Faye and my crow sickness, Joe went to talk to her about what had happened to me, to blame her, but instead he fell in love with her. It seemed that every townie, every one of the boys at the harbor, had talked about falling for her, even as they understood that she was on a different plane from them. They fantasized about something quick, seeded their dreams on her image. But Joe Peavey fell in love. We shared a disorder of the blood that made us partial to whiskey, hard weather, and mermaids.

★   ★   ★

I have nothing to say to you," I said to Faye, who stirred the fire with a brass poker. She flashed me a look, the light glancing off her eyes, and then went over to the sofa and sat down. She wore jeans and a soft baggy sweater the color of an eggplant, her black hair caught loosely behind her head. She tossed her hair over her shoulder, a thick smooth mass that lay there like a glossy stole.

"I'm here only on account of Joe Peavey," I said, "Joe, who is going into his third night in a tree because of his love for you."

The fire snapped and popped. The room was warming up. I wanted to take off my coat. I unbuttoned it. A bead of sweat worked its way earthward down the bumps of my spine.

"He wants you to come out to tell him you love him," I said, "which you don't, but which I wish you would say for his sake. He is high in a tree and, like me, he cannot fly."

Slowly she crossed one leg over the other. She looked sympathetic and sorrowful when I had expected derision and scorn or, at the least, coldness. What were the likes of Joe Peavey and me to one with her power?

"I am sorry about Joe," she said. She had a husky voice, a voice with sandpapery edges, as though she was a heavy smoker and drinker, though she was neither. "But you know it wouldn't do him any good for me to go out there."

She watched me closely. I had the impression that she could see me sweating. I watched her hands: One lay in her lap, long and slender and still, and the other was moving on the back of the sofa, the way a cat's tail will move even when its owner is asleep: independent, stealthy, secret. On her wrist were three silver bangles, and they jingled gently, like chimes.

"The question is," she said softly, scratchily, "what should you do?"

I pictured Joe Peavey in his tree. The moon, as sharp and delicate as a talon, would be rising over the ocean, the hills, and the field, followed by its companion planet. The moon's larger, unlighted section would be cradled in the sliver of light. Joe himself would be a silhouette in the tree. He would be shivering. He would be wondering why he was so high and so alone, yet believing that Faye could love him, given time, given the smallest of miracles, given answered prayers, given a universe whose workings acceded to the wishes of men.

Could I convince Faye to go out to the field? The cottage was warmer than ever. I moved away from the fire, closer to the sofa. I had a flashlight in the car and a long, stout rope; we could rescue Joe. The heat made my cheeks burn.

"You look tired," said Faye.

I was tired. I was tired of standing, of resisting the urge to sit beside her on the sofa.

"I've been working hard," I said.

A shadow of a smile crossed her mouth and played with the light from the whiskey-colored fire rippling across her face.

"You always did," she said.

"Come out to see Joe Peavey with me," I said. My knees were beginning to quiver. With my right knee, I touched the edge of the sofa. "I don't know what will happen to him if we don't go out there."

"Cook, sit down here," she whispered. "I've been meaning to talk to you. I should have talked to you long ago." Her hand moved on the back of the sofa as though hovering, waiting.

Sitting on the sofa was bliss. I felt at home again. My backside relaxed and nestled into the giving pillows. The relaxation spread down my thighs, my legs, my feet, up my sides to my shoulders and arms. Warmth from the fire lapped me, warmed me like liquid fire poured into my bloodstream. In that position, the nagging problem of Joe Peavey in the tree was somehow distanced. As I leaned forward to take off my coat, Faye's hands acted at once: They slipped down my arms and grasped my lapels and maneuvered the coat off me. She stood up, walked with the coat to the coat rack by the front door, hung it up, and came back over to sit beside me, closer than before. She was a stunning sight, a stunning scent, like apples on a cold day, and my pulse began to charge through my body at the thought of the possibilities the evening portended. Joe Peavey could wait.

"I don't love him," she whispered. "You know that. I know that. He even knows that, somewhere in that heart. He's acting like a fool."

The fire crackled. A log settled and sparks showered down.

"You go back out there, Cook," she whispered. "You tell him for me." Her left hand was suddenly resting on my arm, then on top of my hand. "Tell him that it's no good. He's not for me. I'm not for him."

She reached her hand upward and laid her cool fingertips against my cheek. Every hair on my body was electrified. The bangles rang. The fire crackled. Her eyes reflected the firelight. I reached my hand out and felt for her and found her, soft, warm, full, supple, and before I was absorbed into Faye, there in front of the fire, there on the sofa, there on the Oriental rug with the firelight radiating from the brass of the fireplace implements, I felt the triangular tip of her tongue running up the bumps on my spine in the opposite direction of the bead of sweat.

I had been absorbed by Faye for a second time, but this time there was no redemption, no resurrection, no rescue. We slept in each other's arms. The fire died. She built it back up. I tried to move, to help, but she placed her forefinger on my lips. It was like touching me with a wand that rendered me paralyzed. We spent the night there in front of the fire. She released my body from its paralysis, but she held my mind, my heart. She told me with her body that Joe was meaningless to her, that I was everything. Perhaps I had been wrong: It was more than a spell. We would spend our lives together, had, in fact, spent a lifetime together already, a lifetime in one night. We would live by the fire and Joe Peavey would fly from our minds. We pressed our warm skin together and the night swept by, a night like a wind overhead and a fire inside.

Then it was dawn. Dawn—gray, eyes baggy, lips pursed, sober, chastening—looked in the window. A wind rustled against the glass. I looked out and saw the forms of leftover oak leaves working in a breeze against the sky and the shadow of a bird flying away. The fire was dead. I lay curled on the rug, naked, freezing, a few ashes like down on my legs. Faye was not beside me.

I gathered my clothes up from the floor. I walked like a man who had been turned into a chair by a spell and went into her room.

"Faye," I said. She lay on her back. Her eyes opened.

"Why didn't you tell me you were getting into bed?" I staggered into my jeans, shirt, socks, shoes.

She considered me from the covers. Her eyes looked clear, unmuddled by sleep.

"I didn't want to wake you," she said.

"You could have thrown a blanket over me," I said, rubbing my hands. "Look, I've got to go." Asking her to come with me to find Joe would be less than useless. "Will you be here when I get back?"

She pulled the covers up to her nose. Her hair was spread like black fluttering wings on the pillow.

"I'll be here," she said from under the covers, her eyes on mine.

Catapulted from the nuzzle of the warmth into stone-cold dawn, I flew to my car through the drift of leaves. The door slammed shut and made me jump. I twisted around to look from some fear. The cottage looked back, dark and cold. I had pierced Joe, betrayed the one who had saved me. Try as I could, I could not shift the world and turn the blame on Faye. The blame was mine.

I sped down the roads and jumped out of the car and hit the path that led to the field running. By the time I reached the edge of the field that lay before the tree that Joe had climbed, it was full gray light edged with brass at the seaward horizon. Long clouds like fingers stretched over the sky. Even from the edge of the field, I could see that Joe was not in the tree. Had he gone home? Had he happened on a small epiphany during the night that relieved him of his dreadful delusion? Had he climbed down? Had he come down to earth, to his senses?

I sprinted down the rows of corn stubble, ran, ran at a speed that betrayed my betrayal, a speed that said I was too late, that I should never have left my friend in the tree.

Crows were gathered in the top of Joe Peavey's tree. Joe himself lay in the coppery grass beneath it, splayed as if he was out to make angels in the snow, even though he had chosen the wrong season. The crows yelled at me from their high roost, but they didn't fly away. It was their territory, and they were reclaiming it. They were angry, maddened by this interloper, and now me.

"Joe," I said, sucking for air as I approached.

He opened his eyes and turned his head to me.

"Cook," he said. "What time is it?"

"Early," I said.

He laughed.

"So," he said, pushing himself up on one elbow. He yawned. He looked at the tree trunk, then up at the flock of crows cawing and flapping in the treetop. "They've been like this every night since I got in this tree. Driving me buggy."

"It's their roost," I said. "They sleep up there at night. You okay?"

He stretched and yawned again.

"Yeah, yeah. Fine."

"I thought you fell. I thought you were dead."

"No, old friend, but I almost fell, my legs got to quaking so hard. When you didn't come back, I figured it was over. So I climbed down. I was so tired, I had to lie down for a while." He looked around. "Guess I overslept."

I squatted beside him in the grass. The crows kept up their racket.

"I've got something to tell you," I said, looking down the rows of stubble.

Joe Peavey was squinting upward. "Look at them," he said. "You'd think I was trying to kill them." He looked at me. "I did a lot of thinking while I was up there, and not just last night. I know something, can admit something to myself, something that I guess I've known all along. She's not coming out to tell me she loves me.

"Because she doesn't," he said.

"Joe," I said, getting my breath back. "I've got something to tell you."

"But the problem is," he went on, speaking low and gently like someone who has decided something difficult, "the problem is, I still love her. And the question is, what do I do?"

"I've got something to tell you, Joe," I said. I stood up.

"Two things," he went on, as though I hadn't said a word. "I've got two choices. One, make her love me. Wait it out. Work away at her. You know, flowers, candy, nice things. Or two, I go away. Gone. I leave and start up somewhere else. Try to get her out of my mind."

"Joe . . ."

He stood up. Bits of coppery grass stuck to his back.

"No, I lied," he said. "There's three things. Maybe there's even four. Maybe there's a million, for all I know.

"Number three: I could kill her." He was looking at me,

smiling. "Number four: I could kill you. Kill you for what you did with her last night, kill her for the same reason."

I stared at him.

"I was there," he said. "I came down out of the tree just before dawn. I went to Faye's place. Walked. Walked and kept walking to walk her right out of me. But I hadn't walked her out of my mind by the time I got to her place. I still had to see. I looked in the window. Faye saw me looking in. She was in bed. We looked at each other. I couldn't bring myself to say or do anything. I went around to the front and peered in. There you were, out by the fireplace, lying there like a skinned raccoon. I went to see. I saw. I was too late. And I kept walking. I kept walking and came back out here because I still had the fifth thing open to me.

"Number five: Jump out of a tree and break my neck."

"Joe, I can't deny it," I said. "I won't deny it. We're both in love with the same woman."

"You're not in love with her," he said. Then he laughed. "It's better for you if you're not in love with her. She only wants someone around who's not in love with her."

Before last night, I would have agreed. But now I wasn't sure. Now I was beginning to believe that I was in love with her, truly in love in some way I had never believed I would be in love with anything or anybody. All I was thinking of was going back to her place and burrowing with her under the warmth of the covers. I wanted to ask her what she thought of seeing Joe peering in her window at dawn. Would she laugh? Curse? Keep her silence?

I remembered what had seemed the shadow of a bird, flying away as I woke on her floor.

I was suddenly filled with revulsion at Joe. Was this my friend, someone who peered in windows and then, stung, sneaked off to jump into an eternity of self-pity? Someone who was so arrogant and presumptuous to claim to know what Faye wanted? "She only wants someone around who's not in love with her," he

had said. Garbage. It was nothing but simple, ugly jealousy. I was
beginning to reverse my feelings: What Faye and I had done was
the crystallization of our love, such as it was. I was not under a spell.
As an act of love, it would stand. I owed nothing to Joe Peavey.

Toward the sea, a few smoky beams of sunlight fanned sideways through the cloud cover.

I laughed.

"This is fine," I said. "This is truly fine. What I say to you
is true. I am in love with her. I have never stopped being in love
with her. You can climb as many trees as you like, but she will
not love you." I laughed. I laughed in his face. Kill me? Kill
Faye? Never.

"She will never love you," I said.

I turned and struck off down a row. Faye was all I wanted.
To hell with Joe. He could go hang himself, as far as I was con-
cerned. The crows were yelling. I was walking as fast as I could. I
wanted to get to Faye before she stopped wanting me. I had to
hurry. I was in the middle of the field when I realized I had so
much more to tell Joe. I wanted to tell him how much I despised
him for trying to save me the first time, back in the duck-hunting
camp when I wanted to die, should have died and only died
enough to hurt. How much I hated him for falling in love with
the woman I was in love with but who shunned me. How I
cringed with embarrassment for his acting like a village idiot by
climbing the tree and having his name and Faye's splashed all
around town. I wanted to tell him more, that he was spineless,
voiceless, heartless, hopeless. But there was only one way to say
all those things.

I stopped and turned. He stood by the tree, diminished, the
crows flying back and forth above the tree, jeering at him. He
hadn't moved since I had walked away.

Cupping my hands around my mouth, I yelled with as much
force and violence as I could: "CAW CAW CAW! CAW CAW

CAW CAW!" I saw him look and stare. It was all I wanted to say, all I needed to say to finish with Joe. And with the calls, I felt the feathers of my wings spread and I flapped upward and banked and flew to Faye.

———○——

PALS

The short, scrawny one with the S-shaped scar on his chin got out of the car on the passenger side, left the door open, so the buzzer kept buzzing, and jumped down from the pier onto the fantail of my boat.

Looking down at me, he said with a snaky sort of smile, "Hey, chief, you seen Kavner around?"

Behind him on the pier, the big one got out, maybe because he couldn't stand that buzzing, and stood with his arms folded over his gut, which pressed the buttons of his shirt out so hard, they showed through his windbreaker. He wore sunglasses even though an icy mist gusted in off the Sound. His black hair, sparse and stringy, was slicked down over his bald spot but didn't do much to cover it up.

I was toting two five-gallon buckets filled with bilge water. When the car pulled up, I was on my way to empty them in the drums up by the shanties where the town wants us to dump our dirty oil instead of in the harbor. My automatic bilge was busted, something wrong with the impeller, and I'd spent the day up to my armpits in cold slop, bailing and trying to figure out what's what. Missed a trip because of it, and just when the codfish had moved inside.

Now I had this guy on my boat uninvited, his pal up on the dock looking like he wanted to eat someone, and the buzzer buzzing.

"Get out of my damn way," I said, taking a careful step forward so I didn't slop the bilge water on the deck. "And get off my damn boat."

The scrawny one giggled fast and said, "Now what kind of a way is that to talk, old man? You're Blodgett, right? I asked you a simple question."

"And I'll give you a simple answer," I said, heaving the buckets onto the fantail. A splash of bilge water hit one of his shoes. "Get off my boat or get your swimsuit on."

The big one took a step forward and the scrawny one jerked his head at him.

Then he grinned again, so his scar stretched. He looked back at me. The buzzer still buzzed. The grin disappeared.

"Which one is Kavner's boat?" he said, stepping forward so the toes of his shoes—street shoes, black and pointy—hung out over the deck. "Kavner used to work for you, didn't he, old man?"

I tipped my cap back on my head. The mist was splattering my glasses. I shoved my hands into my jacket pockets. I was getting mighty peeved at this scrawny fellow standing on my boat asking me questions and holding up work I didn't want to be doing in the first place.

"Son, you know how cold that water is today?"

Before I could move, the big one lunged fast as a shark and landed on the fantail. The boat listed in his direction as if we had a load of codfish shifting to the stern.

"Want me to take 'im?" he mumbled, his lips showing red inside.

"No, no, Petey," said the scrawny one. "Not Blodgett. We don't take Blodgett."

To me, the scrawny one said in a fake whine, "Old man, pleeeese will ya tell us now, where's Kavner?"

I figured these animals had no good reason to be after Kavner, even though Kavner was a good-for-nothing himself, but I'd sooner pull my toenails out with pliers than rat on a former crewman of mine.

I said, "He lives behind the kitchen at the Melrose Inn. A little room there."

"Where's that, old man?"

"Since you asked so politely, it's on Main Street, five minutes from here."

I wished I was twenty years younger so I could dump both of these creeps headfirst in the oil drums by the shanties and pound them down with a sledgehammer till nothing but the soles of their shoes showed.

When they finally closed their doors to leave, the buzzing stopped. I gave them the whole time it took for me to empty the buckets before I got into my pickup and went as fast as I could the back way down to the Ship Ahoy Motel, in Chatham, where I knew Kavner rented a room.

He was in number 7, the room on the wing facing Harding Beach Road. I had to knock and pound and kick at the door for five minutes before Kavner's voice, crackly and low, said, "Who the hell is it?"

"It's Blodgett. Two guys are after you."

It took another minute before the door opened a crack. I could smell the booze ooze out.

He didn't say anything for a while, just stood there in the darkness on the other side of the door. Then he said, "What they look like?"

I told him.

"One's named Petey," I finished up with.

The chain rattled off and the door opened on to nothing but blackness, the black of a tomb.

"Turn on a light," I said, edging into the room. "Want me to crack my skull?"

I almost wished he hadn't turned on the light. The bathroom door was open and some stink was coming out. The bedspread and sheets were heaped on the floor.

Kavner had crept back to sprawl on the bed. He was wearing only B.V.D.s and he looked like a corpse, lying there with his eyes closed against the light. He was fat and the color of putty.

When he worked for me, he was a strong-backed, hardworking, hustling kid with thick curly blond hair. But he had turned to a different kind of hustling. Soon he had bootlegged and smuggled and drunk and snorted himself into worthlessness. The fishing boat he'd worked so long to pay off was banished by the harbormaster to a mooring in the outer harbor where only a skinny old jetty stood between his boat and the surf of the Sound. The boat wore a skirt of lime green seaweed in the summer, a band of brown slime and barnacles around the waterline all year round, all because his money went to dope and booze. He wouldn't even shell out enough to pay off his slip fees, he was so hooked. That's how low he had sunk.

"We got to get you out of here," I said.

"Forget it," he said, slurring. He inched his eyes open.

I looked at him. His eyes were glassy and had circles under them the color of mold.

"You ready to die?" I said, surprising myself, but not really, since I knew I had to say something surprising to scare him right out of his skin. It was the first thing that jumped off my tongue. "You *want* to die?"

He lolled his head over at me, then swung those glassy eyes up at mine.

"What do you think, old man? You think I'm ready to die?"

I didn't know what to think, or why everybody was calling

me "old man" all over the place, but I did know that those two guys would find out soon enough where Kavner was.

I came around to his side of the bed. "You're coming with me," I said, grabbing him by his arm. But he flicked me off easier than I'd guessed he would, being all doped and drunk up the way he was. I tried grabbing him again with both hands and he shoved me backward and I staggered into the venetian blinds, which made a sound like shuffled cards.

"Get out, Blodgett. They'll be here soon. They won't be happy to see you if you gave them a bum steer."

"You want to die? Call the cops or something. Go to your boat and hide below. What the hell's wrong with you?"

He smiled, and I saw his teeth were a mossy gray.

"My boat?" he said. "Tell you what. You can have my boat."

He flopped an arm over his eyes. "Get out of here, Hank. My pals are coming. Nothing'll happen to me."

I stood there for a minute looking at him. Then I decided something.

"The hell with you," I said, and sprung for the lamp, ripping it out of the wall, cord and all, plunging the room into blackness, and swung, connecting with something Kavner along the way. The lamp was sturdier than I thought, so I swung out again, connected with another piece of Kavner just to make sure.

"Kavner?" I said. "You okay?"

When he didn't answer, I felt my way into the bathroom and found the light switch.

The wedge of light showed Kavner on the bed, conked out, a gash on his forehead.

"Now we're getting somewhere," I said to myself.

I hefted him over my shoulder. He must have weighed a good two hundred with all that alcoholic blubber on him. He stank like a goat and was clammy with sweat. I hauled him out into the cold mist and dumped him in the back of my pickup. I covered him with a tarp I used to cover the flats of herring we bait our trawl lines with.

His room didn't have a phone, so I ran across the parking lot to the side of the motel, where there was a phone booth, and called Bud, my crewman. I told him to be down at the dock and ready to go offshore for two or three days and gave him a quick rundown of Kavner's troubles. Then I drove back down to the harbor. The whole time I was thinking to myself that if I was in Kavner's place, I wouldn't want anyone busting in and telling me how to live my life, either. I looked in the rearview mirror at the wet heap in the pickup bed, one fish-white foot hanging out in the breeze. A sad sack, that's what he was—good for nothing, not even himself. But I figured if he'd been good enough once to work his tail off for me, he might have a spark under all that muck; maybe all he needed was someone to clear away the muck to get to the spark.

Dark was coming on when I pulled into the parking lot at the harbor. Lights were glowing across the harbor in the mist. Bud's beat-up Dodge Dart was there—but so was another car, parked down on the pier at my slip.

Kavner's pals' car.

With Bud, an ex-Marine, I figured we were an even match for them, so I drove right down the pier and parked beside their car.

Bud was standing on the deck and Kavner's pals were up on the pier, just the way it was when I was talking to them before. In his yellow oilskins and his crew cut, Bud stood there smiling like he'd just found two long-lost buddies. But I noticed he was holding the billy club we use on dogfish that foul up our trawl lines. He had the engine running and the running lights on.

"Come to join the party, Hank?" he yelled over the rumble of the engine as I got out of the truck and walked over to the edge of the pier.

The scrawny one turned and smiled his snaky smile.

"Old man, you got a bad sense of direction," he said. "Where'd you run off to, anyway?"

"There you go asking all those questions and standing in my way again."

His fake snake smile faded. "We don't like being lied to. We just wanted to find our old pal Kavner, and you go and lie to us."

I noticed that big Petey was sniffing around my pickup, and then I remembered Kavner's foot.

"Listen, son, we're heading offshore, and we got bait to stow, so if there's anything you got to say, say it."

Petey was just about to look in the bed of the truck so I did the only thing I could to distract him. I hauled off the hugest, meanest sucker punch I could at the scrawny one, not expecting to catch anything but air.

I caught him square on the ear with the meat of my fist. He tried to duck but only jerked and slid a foot out sideways as if he was trying to step on a fleeing cockroach.

Two, no *three* things happened all at once: Petey leapt for me, Bud bounded up from the fantail to the dock, and the scrawny one yelled, "Hold it. For Christ's sake, hold it!"

Everyone froze, Bud holding the club above Petey's head, Petey staring at me through his dark glasses, his stringy hair slicked down and unmussed. The scrawny one clapped a hand to his ear, took it away, and looked at blood.

It wasn't until then that I noticed Petey was holding a knife with a triangular six-inch blade.

"Smart move, old man," said the scrawny one, still looking at the blood cupped in his hand. "Petey, get in the car."

They backed up to their car, the scrawny one staring at me.

He said, "We'll be back for you, old man. We'll be back." Then they slammed their car doors, backed up, and screeched off into the gloom.

"You sure coldcocked him, Hank," said Bud, chuckling. "All he's hearing is bells."

I told him to load Kavner into one of the bunks below so we could get underway.

"That guy's a load and a half," he said after he dumped him below and we shoved off.

An hour later, pounding through the rips in the dark off Rose and Crown Shoal and the rain mixed with sleet that had now begin to come down in sheets, I told Bud to go below to check on Kavner.

"Get some coffee in him. I didn't go through all that trouble for him just to have a snoozehound aboard."

Two seconds later, Bud peered up through the companionway at me.

"Hank, something's wrong."

"Oh, yeah, yeah. The pump." I told him about the bilge pump, that the impeller was busted and we'd have to use the hand pump till I could jury-rig something.

"No, something wrong with Kavner."

"Something wrong like what?

"Like he's not moving. Like he's dead or something."

"You're kidding."

He didn't say anything.

I told him to take the helm. I went below and looked at Kavner. He was staring at the ceiling, the glassiness gone out of his eyes. They were dry and cold as hard-boiled eggs.

I won't tell you what I said to myself.

"Jesus," I said when I got topside and took the helm again. "He's a stiff, all right." I told Bud about clonking Kavner with the lamp so I could get him out of the room. We were steaming along into blackness, taking steep five-foot seas, with a corpse as cargo.

No good deed goes unpunished ran through my mind. A wave

broke over the bow, dousing the windshield, where the one wiper was flailing to no purpose at the rain and spray.

"What're we going to do with him?" said Bud. "Dump him overboard?"

The boat lurched and rolled. Another wave washed over the prow and smashed against the windshield.

I hung onto the helm as we took another sea. I looked out at the sudsing window and the blackness beyond. No one, not even Kavner's pals, let alone Kavner himself, deserved being heaved overboard like a bucket of fish guts into that mess.

I looked at Bud. "Yeah, we are going to dump him overboard. But we're going to do it the right way."

Bud opened his mouth to say something. I knew what it was. His face said it: Bury him at sea in weather like this? Stand out on deck and let the waves get at us? But the look on his face changed. He was a Marine, after all. *Semper Fi.* He knew about the right way of doing things.

I put the automatic pilot on to let it deal with the seas. Maybe it could do a better job than I was doing. We went below and put on all our foul-weather gear, sou'westers included. Then I got Kavner by the feet and Bud got him underneath the armpits. We bashed him so much carrying him topside that if he hadn't been dead to begin with, he sure was by the time we got him onto the afterdeck. I told Bud to grab the tarp that we had covered the bait with so I could wrap Kavner up in it. It wasn't the white shrouds we'd used to wrap guys up when I was in the Pacific during the war, but it was something.

Kavner was rolling around on the deck so much that the minute we'd get him wrapped up, he'd roll right out of it, bare to the storm, white as cheese. So I told Bud to forget it. Bud bunched up the tarp and held on to it so the wind wouldn't snatch it away. The water beaded up on Kavner. I wedged my knee under the rail for support, casting one eye on the sizzling gray-and-white seas and the black flaklike clouds flying overhead. Then I clasped my hands in front of me and bowed my head, solemn and religious.

"Dear God Almighty," I yelled above the wind. The wind tugged at my hat and the rain clattered against my face. "We're here to give you Kavner, a man who wasn't half so stupid as he sometimes acted." I spotted a swell that was running up midships on us. It looked like it might take us hard.

"We thank you, Lord, for not letting those scumbags get this man, and we pray that you'll see to it that Kavner makes up for being a dumb bastard by doing some good works for you up in heaven."

The swell was bigger than I'd been able to make out in the gloom. I yelled to Bud to hold on as it broke. It crashed and swamped the deck, ten tons of bottle green water. I heard the engine bog down with the weight as we yawed and wallowed through the trough. The water rose to my knees, squeezing them hard with pressure, and then ran around them as though I was standing in rapids. I thought that maybe God felt that he'd been mocked by this little ceremony and had decided to take us along with Kavner. But then the water began running out the scuppers. The engine caught up with itself. When the deck cleared, Kavner bobbed up and settled to the deck on the other side of the boat. Bud spat out a jet of seawater. The tarp had vanished.

But it wasn't over yet. The boat made a sharp pitch, rolling Kavner toward us. I jumped up and let him roll underneath my feet, but Kavner steamrollered Bud. Bud went down and slammed against the rail, hitting his head with what sounded like a hammer blow. Then he got a faceful of Kavner as the body slapped into his arms. At first, I thought Bud would be my second victim of the day, the way he lay there holding his hand against his head, his eyes closed. But then he shoved Kavner aside and sat up.

"Can we get this thing over with, Skip?" he said.

I grabbed Kavner by the ankles and hauled him off Bud.

"Okay," I said. "Let's do it."

We manhandled Kavner to the top of the rail and pinned him there on the brink.

"God," I yelled. "I've got only one thing more to say. You've got to go a little easier on a guy like Kavner when he's still alive. Give the guy a break. And the scumbags he got himself wrapped up with? They're the ones who should be here now. Do me one favor, God. Give those goddamn guys hell." I looked at Bud. "Anything you want to add?" He rolled his eyes. So I looked seaward for the next wave. And when the starboard rail went down and we went up, I yelled all I could remember from those other burials: "I commend thee to the sea. Amen." We heaved and Kavner rolled and flopped overboard. With the engine rumbling and the rain and sleet clattering on our hats and the waves racing and rising around us, you couldn't even hear the body make a splash. All you could see was some suds rushing by in our wake.

The boat rolled and pounded into another huge sea. Bud made a move forward and I started to go, too. I yanked the pilot-house door open and stood back to let Bud in first.

As he ducked into the pilothouse out of the weather and I stepped in and closed the door, I clapped him on the back.

"Well," I said, "at least his pals didn't get him."

EVEN THE MOON
SLEEPS

An oblong yellow moon floats above the rip; I bite the end of the flashlight so both my hands will be free. The boat wallows. The beam flashes over the scabbed, flaking paint of the deck and rail and for a moment illuminates the snowy foam of a comber passing out of the rip beside us. The wave flips hand-shaped blobs of foam into the air.

I must hurry; we are close. There is a smell in the air, a reminiscence of watermelon. I must think methodically, force fluid thought through the cement of fatigue. I direct the beam into the white plastic bucket sitting on the lid of the fish box.

"Smell 'em?" says Turk, invisible at the stern, his voice telegraphing an uncharacteristic excitement. "They're here tonight."

At the bottom of the bucket, coils of black-green eels glisten in the beam of my flashlight. It is impossible to tell one apart from the other, to make heads or tails of the mass, where one starts and another ends. Revulsion washes over me. I must force myself to reach in and get one. It is hard to force myself, but it is easier now, being tired and heavy as lead, moving mechanically. I do not even have to tell myself not to think about it: The revulsion means nothing, passing fast as a comber.

The boat heaves. I grab a burlap bag and reach in and feel and the eels lurch and writhe out of my grasp. They are amazingly swift. Any hesitation on my part is their escape. One's too fat; another's too skinny. I grab one by the middle and it muscles free. I clamp down on one behind its head, saliva trickling out of the sides of my mouth around the end of the flashlight. The head is the only place to get purchase. I lift the eel as it twists spasmodically from its mass in the bucket and it coils around my arm. It tries to hunch its head backward out of my fist, its eyes staring in the flashlight beam, its white lips working. A wave smacks the stern, sprays us; we are closer still. I must hurry.

With my free hand, I bring the hook under its chin and skewer it through its nose. It sends a jolt through the eel and I feel the animal tense around my arm. Then I peel the eel from my arm and lift eel and hook and wire line and move to the stern rail, letting the hooked, dancing eel swing outboard so it will not twist around the line. An eel can knot itself around the line, tie itself into a sheepshank.

I remove the flashlight from my cramping jaws, shut it off, and stuff it in the pocket of my down vest. I set the bucket on the deck and stuff the burlap over the eels. I blink and pick up my fishing pole, which has been resting in the corner where the stern and port rail join, and I stand at the stern rail.

I blink again and Turk materializes at the tiller, with his own fishing pole jutting from his hip like a yardarm against the tilted moon schooning above the rip behind him.

"Ready?" is all he says, and I say yeah and begin letting out wire line from the big reel, feeling it slither out under my thumb, letting my calluses watch for any kinks. A kink in the wire equals a lost bass. Turk throttles up and turns the tiller with his thigh as he lets out his own line, bringing the boat broadside to the lead breakers of the rip, where the tide meets a sudden rise in the seafloor and the seas roil.

Standing at the stern, away from the engine, we can speak in normal voices and hear the unsettling surging, seething waves of the rip. I think of sailing vessels, or any ship aground, its engine dead: This is the sound they hear in disaster. I try looking directly at the rip, but when I look just away from it, I can pick it up more clearly in my peripheral vision, a trick of the light at night.

We troll just beyond this tumult, in the glass-smooth water being drawn into the rip like a half-mile-wide sheet of newsprint. With the racing tide, our eels swim our hooks into the submarine churn of this rip, where troops of striped bass patrol for food, these tiny Atlantic eels like lost apostrophes swimming in the blackness, nearing the lead bass, swimming away from the pain in their mouths toward a black hole.

We take one pass at the rip, all tension, fists on poles, eyes wide to admit night's light, every neuron awaiting the first hit. No hit comes. Turk steers the boat so that the moon is now over him, our wire lines extending into the whitecaps like threads spun from spume. If I lean just so, wedged into the corner where the starboard rail meets the stern, I can angle over the sudsy wake and feel as though I alone am floating above the water, like a flying soul hunting the wastes for a passageway to heaven.

My eyes are now adjusted to the darkness and I can see our wake, all cold, fiery phosphorescence, and I can make out the ghost shadows of seabirds flapping above the rip on a nighttime slaughter of the bait fish caught in the sea below. I must think *bass, bass, bass,* be ready for the hit.

"Lot of fire in the water," says Turk.

Have I been asleep or awake? I have not been ashore in days. At the end of this trip, there will be a handsome paycheck, as handsome as this business affords a journeyman afterdeckman, but as I try to calculate the share I have taken bassing aboard this boat, hauling lobster gear on another boat two days before, filling in for another crewman on a long-lining boat the week before that, the numbers jumble.

Lot of fire in the water," Turk has said, and I begin to form words that respond to his statement. Good thing there's a moon, I think I will say; it kills the fire. But I am not sure whether I have said it. When the moon's down, there'll be too much fire, I think I will say; the bass will see the line. But I am not sure I have said it.

Water sizzles by the stern as we take our S-shaped course along the front of the rip. I shift my stance, and as I shift, the strike comes.

Strike.

No more thought. I have a hit.

Strike and I'm on. A fish is on. The pole bends; the lunging weight is in my hands. There is no mistaking the hit of a hungry big striped bass. A hit is like getting snagged by a dark fast-running express train, the unseen hand of an underwater giant presence yanking at the end of the line. The pole bends; the weight from beyond begins to strip line from the reel. I have blurted, "Fish!" before I know it. The fish is running and the pole is nodding and Turk flips the boat out of gear so that we can drift with the fish, one strong, hale striped bass harnessed by a hook leading us stern-first into the rip.

The sound of the waves grows nearer, a low roar, a high hiss. Before us, the mist from the churning waters rises around the moon. The reel whines. The cries of seabirds spear the air. Focus has returned to my fatigue-logged brain; it is a waiting focus, a tension, as taut as the line leading into the waves. I concentrate on this feeling of connection to a fish with fight and strength that is sending life into me, like a transfusion of energy. This wonderful fish! Strike the eel with a decisive force and discover in rage the hidden hook! Run, run away from this pain, this other force that turns its head and pulls it where it does not want to go. Never before has this fish been told what to do. It has never been *done to;* it has always done the doing.

The fish runs. We are nearing the first curling breaker of the face of the rip. I am electrified. I hunger to begin reeling back, to control the boundings of the fish, but I must be patient, let the fish run. How well is it hooked? Will it shake the hook and shun the eel? Leave me with a sprung reel and a curse on my tongue? Speed off into its submarine reaches to remain unreachable?

The steadily breaking wave looms; we approach, rise in our approach. The roller-coaster ride is about to begin. Turk has reeled in and stowed his pole and grabbed the long gaff, and now we both stand with knees locked against the stern rail as the stern rises, rises, and with a stiff lurch the boat meets the breaker. A gasp of water overfalls us and we are soaked. The action of the boat has changed: It is tumult; it is riot. Turk obliterates the moon as the boat heels upward; the next moment, on the downswing, the moon appears out of his silhouetted head like a magic coin trick.

In the rip, we gain the advantage on the sprinting fish. Already, the fish telegraphs its tiredness into my hands, begins taking less line. It is weary of the pain and the burden. Nothing tires an animal not made for carrying burdens more than a burden carried in fear and anger. This fish is carrying steel line, me, the boat. It is a big fish. This I know from the gauge of the pole, the angle of its curve a register of its weight.

Bounced and battered, the boat drifts through the rip, moon-silhouetted birds fluttering over us, past the moon, the pop-up waves exploding beside us, acres and acres of ocean in battle with itself. But even in this wild ride, I tentatively draw the pole upward, taking the pulse of the fish. It turns, then bolts again, taking more line. Then suddenly, everything stops and the line goes slack.

"Aw shit," I hear myself say.

"What?"

I begin reeling hard and, by my reeling, Turk has an answer to his own question.

I reel madly, guiding the backing in, then the steel line, bearing down, my guts sinking not from the bounding of the boat but from an expectation of disappointment. And suddenly, the weight is there again; the fish has turned and run toward the boat, carrying slack line toward me: The hook has not come free.

"Got him," I say, slowing now, pumping the pole easily, working in the exhausted fish, once again in control. Now I can concentrate on keeping my balance as the boat runs the gauntlet of the rip, the moon rocks in the sky.

I see him," says Turk. "There."

The bass is close. This is the tight time, the time of palpitations and caught breath, when a devilish wave, the hand of the counterforce, can take the fish in its hands and pull it free, when the shank of the hook can bend, the barb break, when fishermen curse the name of Mustad but really understand the hook is not at fault, that the unseen submarine hand is.

I reel more carefully but not too slowly, steadily, calculating a path between the pop-up waves, bringing the pole to the left to guide the fish around to the starboard rail where Turk can get a clean swipe with the gaff. The fish surfaces in a white wake, sounds, surfaces closer. I see a sudden flash of stripes and a gaping mouth.

Turk, cat-quick, is up on the transom, gaff cocked. I take two more turns on the reel. Everything is in Turk's hands now. I ease the pole forward, bringing the fish closer. Turk leans toward the fish just as a pop-up takes the stern and shoves it moonward. Turk swings the gaff and hooks the fish. The fish lunges, splashing and thrashing, but Turk has the gaff in. He grunts and heaves; the fish is out of the water and on the rail, and then the fish hits the deck with a thump, splattering scales like priceless coins.

"Yes!" I say, and Turk has already returned to the tiller, jammed the throttle open, and steers the boat back on a course through the rip.

I set my pole down and take out my flashlight. The fish glitters its pajama stripes in the glare, this fresh, gasping forty-pound striped bass with its regal green-and-silver stripes. No fish-market dullness in its magnificent coat of armor. I grasp the line and work the hook free, the fish too exhausted to fight except for a brief flurry with its spread fantail and a few displays of its spined and ordovician dorsal fin. I extract the hook and find that the eel is still attached and twistingly alive, a Jonah eel, spat out from the stomach of its own leviathan.

We have burst out of the rip and returned to the smooth water before I have hefted the fish up and laid it down in the fish box, this one fish worth the price of the trip in fuel and food.

Turk steers the tiller with his thigh and lets his line run out. He is radiating a fierce eagerness, switching his head this way, then that, watching the birds, glancing at the moon, which is now visibly lower and going orange. He thirsts for bass; he wants to make money, but he wants to fight them, win, feel the feeling that I am feeling, the feeling that drives you to get your line out faster and hope that your eel is the chosen eel. But even as I let out my lucky eel again, I feel the cement of exhaustion setting around my joints and my mind.

"Big bass," I say.

And looking into the rip, Turk says, as if challenging the water to yield bass to him, "There's more in there."

★　★　★

Two weeks offshore, nearly three, without a break. I am punchy. Only once in two weeks have I been ashore for a longer time than it takes to fill the fuel tanks. I remember the situation, not the day or week, days and weeks being too fluid to grasp. But still I remember: It is two o'clock or maybe three in the morning. I am ashore. From somewhere across the harbor, a dog is barking. I walk from the boat, the *Dauntless,* the long-liner, my legs feeling small and short and withered, as if they have shrunk offshore.

A damp southwester is blowing, tinkling through the halyards of the tourists' sailboats. The air is thick with moisture laden with the smell of seaweed, so that around the streetlight hangs a green halo.

In my T-shirt and jeans and torn moccasins, I stand by the phone booth, the macadam of the parking lot rocking underfoot, and think, *It is good to feel the land.*

In the background, I can hear the diesel of the *Dauntless* idling. The deck lights are on, we're almost ready to head back offshore, and I am heading with them on back-to-back trips long-lining for codfish on the Northern Edge. Already we have spent four days in a wilderness of fog a hundred miles from land, and now we are heading into another four.

I see the figures of the crew moving about on the afterdeck of the *Dauntless.* Two o'clock, maybe three: It is too late to call anyone. I don't have enough time to go home to get fresh clothes. So I stand and smoke a cigarette, and then I amble down the solid dock, my equilibrium taking into account phantom seas, and go back to my endless job.

The moon is a half slice of cantaloupe about to be swallowed by the sea. Turk has hooked one and lost one, hooked another and boated it. I have boated another, but the tide is going slack, the rip is dying, and soon the fire in the water will tip off the striped bass that the eels they pursue have hidden hooks, that they must move on to richer rips, inexorably heading south through the last warmth of the year of these early days of September, seeking eels elsewhere in the offshore rips, to the east and south and behind Nantucket, in Orion and Tomahawk and Asia Rip, and then strike south across the distances and depths for the shallows of the Chesapeake.

We reel in. The last fin of moon rides the ocean beyond Nantucket and then is gone. It has slipped into its dark bedchamber beyond the rim of the earth. And I feel beneath my exhaustion a sudden subtle excitement, a different excitement from the fishing excitement: I will soon be stepping ashore. Thankfully, there is no other job on the horizon. I will shower and sleep and sleep some more, and in a few days I will emerge from my cottage to blink at the light and saunter into town, drink a few cold beers, look up some buddies, drink a few more cold beers, and then, and only then, begin to look for another slot on a boat.

Turk finishes reeling in and hands me his pole.

"Only three fish," he says, opening the lid of the fish box. "I'll have to go back goddamn codfishing at this rate."

He lets the lid slam down and goes forward and flips on the pilothouse light.

Now that we will head for home, my internal barometer has changed: It soars and sends a surge of excitement at the prospect of the feel of solid ground under my feet, of dry, clean clothes, of hot food on a stationary plate, of a solid, firm bed, a pillow. I think of a warm, unmoving bed as I begin hosing down the deck.

Turk brings the throttle up to cruising speed.

And as I wash down the deck, I think about how for the next two hours I will lie in the sleeping bag below in the bunk, in an approximation of the state of the striped bass we have boated, lie in a near-death flop, enveloped in the roar of the diesel, and I will wake up with the dawn a hint of pastel in the sky on the other side of the creamy dunes of Monomoy Island, knowing that within the hour I will be walking jelly-legged across the dock, headed toward bed.

As I busy myself with the poles, I see Turk looking at a chart. He opens the tide book, looks back at the chart, checks his wristwatch, looks back at the tide book. I secure the bucket of eels under the transom and try not to let myself believe what I think he is doing.

I do not want to be stuck offshore, consumed by exhaustion, banished to an endless series of sleepless nights and days aboard pounding boats, a Flying Dutchman unaware of his transgression. Let me go ashore. Give me the chance to sleep, please. Give me the chance to clear my head! Even the moon has a chance to sleep; why can't I?

Turk appears in the pilothouse door, a looming shadow, as I come forward to stow the poles below.

And his silhouette, leaning against the doorway, says to me, "Just leave those topside. I want to head down below Nantucket, give it a shot down there."

He turns, disappears into the bright pilothouse, then suddenly reappears, a head leaning out of the light.

"You didn't have any plans, did you?"

HOW ARE YOU TODAY?

*Sailors
ride
heaven's winds
taking ships
to distant
places
like birds
in the clouds
gone without a trace*

—Li Po

How are you? she thinks as she stares out through the windshield at the sea. *How are you today?*

This is not beach weather. It is frigid. It was about ten degrees when I left the house, and it has not gotten any warmer. Not that it should. It is about three-thirty in the afternoon, and it will be dark soon. It is overcast. A few snowflakes flutter out of the clouds. The water is dark gray with whitecaps. The wind sends shivers up the backs of the waves. The beach is covered with a thin layer of snow that glows white in contrast with the grays. Beyond the surf, I can see a raft of sea ducks bobbing on the waves. Eiders? Scoters? He would know.

How are you doing today? she thinks. *Is there anything I can get you?*

I am sitting in the cab of the pickup. The wind rocks the truck now and then, spatters sand against the door. Usually, I get out of the truck and walk the beach. There is a sound that the breaking of the little waves makes, when it is calm, that makes me think that the world is a true place and that it is not a shell over a massive super-structure that has decayed so with rust and neglect that it could disintegrate at any moment and the shell could fall in on itself. What would be left? Dust.

Today, it is too bitter to walk the beach.

Once, I stood up on the roof of the cab to look out at the horizon. I could see his boat as it headed toward Monomoy Point. I watched as it steamed away. On that late-summer day, the day, the last day seven months ago, the sun was warm and the light was gold, slanting from the west. The sea was a rich shade of blue, like the pattern on our old china. The dunes of Monomoy were a line of spilled cream and the winds were flat, calm, peaceful. I watched his boat depart. Soon it was a speck of white. I looked away; above me, a sea gull had dropped a mussel to the parking-lot pavement right beside the truck. When I looked back, there was nothing but blue.

Once, I walked the tide line in a fog beyond which there was no world. I strained to hear the drone of my husband's boat. The scent of seaweed was sweet, the splash of waves like marbles shaken in a sock. The beach stretched in a blur only a few feet ahead, and then there was fog. Ahead, a figure formed: a ghost. But it was no ghost. As it came nearer, it materialized into an old man. His face was suddenly so near, so definite, that I could see the broken blood vessels in his crooked nose, the cataracts in his eyes. He wore an old beaten khaki golf cap and a navy blue windbreaker, baggy khaki pants over his bowed legs, and torn Top-Siders. He touched the brim of his hat with two fingers as we passed. I took three steps, then turned around to look. He was not there. Only the beach and the wall of fog stood behind me. I looked around, surrounded by the fog. I strained to hear the engine, the thudding of the diesel. *The fog should amplify sound,* I thought. I walked onward, found the jetty. I bounded over the slick rocks to the end of it and held my breath. And then, there it was, a distant, nearly vanished murmur. The world did exist beyond the fog, and there was the sound of my husband's boat to prove it.

When our daughter was born, I did not go to see my husband off to sea as I did every trip he took, every season, every hour on the clock. I thought it would be wiser to stay at home. But when my husband left for the harbor to head to sea, I paced the house with the baby in my arms and kept stopping to look out the windows of our house: the yard, pines, oaks, the grove of locusts, the sandy driveway. The windows seemed like clear water. I longed for the glimpse of the boat, the flash of the sun off the pilothouse windows, the white mustache of bow wake, the lonesome running lights as the boat rounded the outer channel markers and set a course for the ocean. Finally, I took the baby. And she came with me every time, every dawn, every afternoon, every night, until she was old enough to decide for herself whether she would come to see her father off to sea.

The leavings and returnings all come back to me. They are unwelcome. I want them to disintegrate, turn to a shower of dust. I want to stop coming to this empty beach to watch the perfect hairline horizon, the soulless waves, the watchful, staring gulls.

How are you today? she thinks, listening to the wind bustle around the truck. *If only I could ask you one more question.*

* * *

The day is darkening. The visibility is immaculate. Everything stands out in sharp relief in this pure light. The snow on the beach glows. The granite waves rise to break on the frozen beach.

Once, I saw a sunrise that so saturated the world with pink light, the few clouds, the ripples on the sand, the individual blades of beach grass, the skin on the back of my hand, that I begged God to select me instead of my husband or my daughter, should he have important plans for them. How I wish my prayer had been answered and how I curse my stupidity at such vanity.

Once, I saw a harbor seal poke its head out of a wave. He looked at me, watching. His huge eyes seemed to be saying that he was waiting for me. If he could speak, would he have invited me in for a swim? He bobbed and watched, his coat glistening. I watched back. And then he dived and was gone.

Once, under the light of a high three-quarters moon, bathed in its blue-edged light as I stood at the water's edge one cold, still night, I watched his boat run to sea. All I could see of the boat were its port running light and stern light, miles at sea, moving away from me as if skimming the water, flying above the surface: red and white. Could I have run along the shimmering path of the moon to meet the boat before it reached the open ocean? The lights vanished. I watched the water sparkle under the moon. I saw a buoy light flashing and a fan of light in the distance from a lighthouse beyond the rim of the horizon. The rustle of wings. And then I turned and walked back up the beach, opened the squeaky door of the pickup truck, and drove home.

Should I see my daughter coming toward me from the beach, right now, at this second, I would fly to her, to hold her, to hold her only and resist the urge to speak—and yet the beach does not change. The beach, with its wind-carved snow cover, and the sea, covering itself quickly, hiding everything it has done, give away nothing. She came to me and stayed with me, forsaking her brimming life for my sake. She stayed beyond the time she could stay no longer. She must have been torn, tugged homeward, and yet she remained, smiling, calm, present. She watched me, helped me, mothered me. But days later, when we were able to talk of watching him go to sea, she wept. I held her as she sobbed and her tears turned the shoulder of my blouse warm and wet. Does she know how her love for me and the life we've shared now makes me gasp with gratitude, how ungrateful I feel to know that what she offered me cannot fill the hollow? And yet, what she gave me is the hope of a beginning. I must go on.

If I could only ask him, she thinks, *if I could only ask him how he is doing, what he needs.*

Tomorrow I will not come to the beach. Tomorrow I will be different. The things that occupy me now at times, I will force to occupy me all the time. I will go to my job. I will read different books. I will eat different food. I will talk to different people. Tomorrow I will be somewhere else, I will take this truck and drive without stopping until I find myself in a place I do not know three hundred miles from here. I will not observe the gulls hanging in the wind as though held in the air on invisible strings. I will not observe the fringe of ice around the jetty, white as an ermine stole. I will not observe this emptiness.

I will drive to visit my daughter. Yes! I will take a vacation from work. No: I will quit work. I will no longer wish I could hear the mudroom door open at some magic hour of the night or smell the sweet smell of a pair of fishing pants steeped in brine and sequined with fish scales. I will no longer wish to feel the touch of his hands as rough and smooth as shingles. No, none of this is my life anymore. I want to erase it all. I do not wish I could ask him how he is.

This is what I will do: I will push aside these seven months. I will take them up in my hand and run to the water and throw them back in. They are sand; they will filter through the water and settle to the seafloor unseen and countless.

At the seaward horizon, the shelf of clouds has come free and now there is a faint sliver of peach light. Light! Seven gulls have landed on the roof peak of the boarded-up changing shed, and all face into the wind. I will leave and not come back. Their feathers are tinged with a faint blush of peach light. I will not wish for him. I will not wish for a ghost. Even the old man I once saw come out of the fog, so many years ago: I will not wish to be there again, in that time, wishing I could hear the engine coming from the world beyond the fog. Did the old man have a message for me? Did I smile at him, or was I too surprised?

I will leave now. The sliver of light at the horizon is broadening. The clouds are beginning to part. I see blue-gray clouds tinged with peach where once I saw only gray overcast, and a hint of pale blue sky between the rows of cloud. I will leave. I will drive right now. I will not even go back to the house. I will put the truck in reverse, back up, put it in gear, and drive away through the night. And when I come to the end of the journey, I will throw my arms around my daughter. Perhaps I will leave this place altogether, forever, take hold of myself and shake.

Snap out of it! he would have said.

I will not be brought to my knees. I will run away from these seven months before they choke me. Running is the first step. I will take the first step. I will stop coming here to this godforsaken beach to look for nothing, to look for the wind. I can no longer breath here. I am suffocating myself in myself!

I crave a new life without memory. I will make one. I will make it up. I will find my own redemption. I will go to my beloved daughter, who is still in this life and within reach, and I will touch her, touch her face, hold her to me, talk with her. I see this new life opening to me, opening like the clouds are opening to the softening light. There is time. I will go this instant!

But before I do, I must have one more time. One more time is all I ask.

Let me ask you, she thinks, her gloved hands gripping the steering wheel. *Is there anything I can get you? How are you today?*